AIN'T NOTHIN'
BUT
A STRANGER
IN THIS WORLD

BRUCE SUDDS

AOS Publishing 2022

ISBN: 978-1-990496-03-5

Cover Design: Rue Mader

Visit AOS Publishing's website:
www.aospublishing.com

This book is dedicated to my first friend, Ian,
for all we've been through together,
and my best friend and partner today,
Carrie, for the same reason...

"...If I ventured in the slipstream
Between the viaducts of your dreams
Where immobile steel rims crack
And the ditch in the back roads stop
Could you find me?
Would you kiss-a my eyes?
Lay me down
In silence easy
To be born again
To be born again
To be born again
In another world, darling
In another world
In another time
Got a home on high
Ain't nothin' but a stranger in this world
I'm nothin' but a stranger in this world
I got a home on high
In another land
So far away
So far away..."

"Astral Weeks"
Van Morrison

The River I Stand In

"Would you like a story?" he asked. "A tale that will grant you peace?"

I paused. "What sort of story?"

Before I go on, I should tell you I needed the words on these pages, but I had resisted them for a long time.

This tale was tired of waiting for me and insisted on its presence. It found me at the bar, sat down, put its boots up on the table, and asked for a drink.

"Grab a glass for yourself while you're at it. You look like you could use one."

Again, I didn't request the intrusion. But I was lost. A change was needed and I was incapable of making it, so it happened to me.

I had a house in Toronto. By all accounts, I was productive. There was one eventful day, and then, in those that followed, my life began to unravel. "Things are going badly, but at least it's happening quickly, and at an increasing speed," I told a friend.

I kept losing stuff. But nothing I wanted to surrender. Just my phone, credit cards at bars, opportunities, and relationships.

I woke up, and the only voicemails and texts were a few days old; from my mom and an old friend. Both just "checking in." The modern way of saying "I'm concerned."

I could often find solace in songs and long walks. After wandering for half an hour with my headphones on and three-quarters of *Astral Weeks* complete, I felt no growing ease or joy.

My Uber driver turned on the radio after my second question and a rant about the conservative government.

And then there was the incident at the bar.

I showed up at the Dora Keogh frustrated. I felt trapped in my circumstances. So, I got drunk.

I was leaning against the bar, texting a friend to come meet me.

Two women were beside me, ordering drinks. Then, a guy arrived. I ignored them, but the tenor of the conversation changed and caught my attention.

"No, you gotta come with me. You're gonna love it. It's gonna be a great party," the man said.

"It's ok. We're going to stay here. We wanna see the band," one of the women replied.

"C'mon!"

"No, thanks."

He put his hand on her arm. I saw her try to move away. From her reaction, I assume he didn't let go, or his grip tightened.

The woman's eyebrows went up, and her tone sounded angry. "Hey, let go!" she ordered.

"Fine."

The two women began to walk away.

As they did, the man threw them a parting jab: "Bitches."

They heard him. "What?"

"I said you're both bitches."

At that point, I decided I should step in.

"Apologize to her," I ordered.

"No. Why?"

"You know why."

The two women were confused but spoke up. "Wait. What?"

"He's going to apologize to you."

"No, I'm not."

"Yes, you are, or we're going outside."

"Sorry, I guess."

The women were confused and understandably annoyed with both of us. One of them spoke up, "Whatever...you two are both psychos."

They left, and I turned to him.

"Do you wanna dance?"

"What?"

"We would feel a lot better if we danced."

"Weirdo."

"Ok."

As I returned to my drink, he pushed me and took a swing. I ducked, then emptied his bottle of beer on his head, and splashed onto his wet face with the back of my hand.

Before I knew it, I was in the arms of a couple of larger guys. It wasn't gentle, but I did sense their restraint. Then I was on my back on Danforth Avenue, resting quietly.

I could blame the whiskey. I tried. But I'm the one who chose both the liquor and its quantity. I knew the amount that would lead me to find the one asshole in the place, and I would make it my job to tell him about his nature. I began to enjoy telling people they were wrong, off-side. Recently, a few whiskeys deep, I walked by a decorative Jameson's mirror at Allen's and saw a reflection of a guy who I knew would be trouble. He had the look. I needed to start talking to him... Yeah, it was me.

You could sense the crash coming if you approached me, and the last thing anyone would want to do is go down with me or even witness it.

When I searched myself, I knew I was a writer. That was something. I had this calling to write, and I couldn't deny it. I wondered if part of the reason I was lost was that I had convinced myself I was a scribbler, but I had no story to tell. I had no success that meant much to me. I had won contracts and awards as a journalist, copywriter, speechwriter, and editor. But when I tried to write a book, I found I quickly exited through the side door. The subjects couldn't hold me.

When I was nearing the bottom of this experience— hopeless, angry, despondent—this story forced its way into my life. I couldn't deny it.

If I'm honest, I will tell you that this tale was always within reach, but I refused to grasp it.

The writer Kurt Vonnegut said that it took him over twenty years to go back to Dresden and compose his book about the fire-bombing of the city where he was a prisoner of the German forces during World War Two. He finally hopped on a plane with a pal from the conflict. His wristwatch began to malfunction as he took off, and he shared his yarn of a man he knew from combat, Billy, who became unstuck in time. The past and present, alien worlds, and peculiar knowledge formed the nexus of his tale. Billy didn't choose what happened to him, but he gave himself over to it. He was honest about it. Billy spoke about his experience even after they tried to put him in a hospital for it.

I was lost, so I did what I had done in the past — I went back to where I grew up and spent time alone outdoors. On this trip, I finally embraced the words I needed to hear. And that is this book.

And now, this is the story I tell myself.

I did check the facts, and they are correct. I have pursued the terrible, mystifying, and sometimes heroic exploits and relayed them as they've been communicated to me. No more. No less.

So, what is this? Is this fiction or nonfiction? All I can answer is that it's true. You may disagree about whether certain events occurred, but I will only tell you that this is written with great sincerity. I have changed the names to allow for the privacy of those within, but the details are correct.

When I think about choosing to write this book, my mind turns to a bridge in Toronto. A river runs through the center of the city. The Don. There is a quote by the ancient philosopher Heraclitus painted on one of the Don's bridges: "This river I step in is not the river I stand in."

"Billy, will you step into the river with me?"

"Of course. I've stepped in far worse."
We hold hands. To secure each other in the current.
We had been tossed out of life, strewn along the banks. To step
back in like this was awkward, our footing unsure, the current
powerful, and the whole affair particularly tricky with a
hangover.

The bright spark of a poet, who lived so short a life,
wrote a line that I've held to for many years; since I was a
teenager. "A man's life of any worth is a continual allegory —
and very few eyes can see the Mystery of his life — a life like
the scriptures, figurative."

My single most significant moment to date as a writer
was when a friend, in his infinite kindness, pulled a slip of
paper from his wallet and handed it to me when I was low. It
read, "the goal of all this writing is freedom. To no longer need
to write. To be free from the compulsion and find peace."

"You left your journal open, and I read that, scribbled
it down on a scrap of paper, and have kept it with me ever
since."

Now that I've heard this chronicle, checked the facts,
and played it over in my mind, this is the truth I hold.

"Wouldn't it be funny," Billy asks me, gripping my
hand more firmly as we stand in the cold, moving waters, "if
the worst thing that happened to us was also a gift, wrapped
in a strange puzzle that was painful to complete?"

"Shut up, Billy."

PART I

"Last Night"
Lightnin' Hopkins

He entered the bar looking weathered. As though he lived a life outdoors. It made sense. When I knew him, he was happiest in the wilds.

There was athleticism and a well-worn quality to him—a bit like a baseball glove used for quite a few seasons. He was in his thirties, with a muscular build, around six feet tall, dark blonde hair, and a slightly tanned complexion. He had a light stubble, and his nose took a slight turn in the middle of the bridge that suggested he'd broken it at some point, and it had never been set correctly.

I had been two days alone in the backcountry of southern Ontario and decided I needed to see people. Here, the Canadian Shield dips down to the south, and a series of lakes and rivers form in the valleys offered between the worn remnants of mountains. I travelled those waters by canoe. I found government lands and provincial parks where I could throw up a tent, far from anyone.

I could fish, read, swim naked day and night, play guitar and not bother or be bothered by anyone. I loved to lay on the warm granite, covered in pine needles and moss. The waters were sweet and black but held no secrets other than smallmouth bass and lake trout. Often, when I am in the city, my mind would turn to trips like this to lift me, and I would be better for it.

At night, alone by the fire, I would gaze into it and find the faces of those I've known and scenes from my life. It would make me miss these people. Wandering away from the flames, I watched the animals out here with me gather together to face the night—families of geese, deer, and raccoons. And here I was: standing alone in the dark. Singing to myself, sharing stories with no one, and sleeping alone. Even the raccoons knew what I still hadn't figured out. I was still out here living my reckless ways.

8

In the morning, I packed up the camp, paddled back to the mainland, loaded the car, and left the wilds behind me.

There was a tavern that I liked to visit that rested along the St Lawrence River. It was an old house transformed into a restaurant with a bar. The place was a home for generations of smugglers, loafers, tourists, and a few drunks. This disparate crowd allowed me to fit in. And I liked them.

He took the stool beside me. The staff seemed to know him. He had an ease about him that could not be ruffled. A placid pond immune to wind or any other sort of turbulence. He was always smiling to himself, it seemed.

"It's been a long time..."

"It has."

"So, what brought you back here?"

"I'm just getting away."

"From what?"

"The city. People. Myself."

I was a few whiskey and sodas into the evening, so I enjoyed being pointed. And maybe he was an asshole that needed someone to tell him that was the case. No, I was done with that, I told myself.

"How's that working out?"

"Poorly. But I'm trying something new today."

"You sound like an artist."

"I'm a writer."
"What have you written?"

"Nothing you would know."

"You sound sad about that."

"I guess I am."

"Why's that?"

"I can't find what I need to write about. None of the stories I try seem to mean much to me."

"I see. Would you like a story? A tale that will grant you peace?"

I paused.

"What sort of story?"

He laughed.

"You're suspicious. That's fine. How about I tell you a bit, and then you decide if I should continue? I can stop at any time. It's up to you."

"Fair enough."

"Do you need a drink?"

"Always. Especially now. But I'll have just one more. I'm trying something new...You?"

"Sure, I'll join you. I mostly come here to talk to people. I only have one drink, maybe two. One or two is lovely. After that, conversation and I begin to suffer and wilt."

"T.B. Sheets"
Van Morrison

"Let's find a quiet spot."

He nodded towards a table in the corner of the bar. We took our seats.

"I will tell you this story, but there is one condition."

"What's that?"

"You can't ask me to explain anything about it. Every good tale is ruined with explanations. It's best if I leave room for you, the audience, to breathe and to move."

"Ok."

"But first a drink."

He turned to the bar and requested two Jameson's, neat.

The bartender brought the drinks to the table. My new companion nodded and smiled at him and then lifted his glass. His face grew solemn as he turned to me.

"To absent friends."

Our glasses clinked.

"Let me begin with something that happened about eighteen months ago. Two people, named Diana and Devin, who hadn't seen each other in nearly thirty years and were separated by thousands of miles, had the exact same experience. This was an intrusion, or echo, of something that occurred when they met as young people. I will have to tell you more about that a little later...

In a small studio apartment above Technosolucions Florez, an electronics store in Carepa, Colombia, Diana Glendon lay doubled over in bed. She was overcome with physical pain and sorrow. She had lost her colleague, likely to a violent death, and she was gravely ill herself. She writhed on the mattress, gasping for air.

"Ooooohhhhh, Victoria, Victoria... I'm so sorry," she moaned.

Diana had an athletic frame, tall and sturdy. Even now, sweating on the bed with her dark blonde hair splayed across the pillow, she looked more spent than ill.

Sobbing, she continued, "I didn't know, Victoria... I didn't know this would happen... Sean." Who is Sean, she thought? Bewildered. Memories formed. Why... Sean... now? And then it happened. She saw it. She was driving a truck, and there were two boys travelling along a road. One was on a bicycle. The other was walking beside him. She was getting closer.

Oh, my God! No!

She could hear voices in Spanish out on the street and the sound of the traffic. The air was hot, stale and humid. She was alone but whispered, "Open up the window. Let me breathe."

She continued to weep. Not out of pain or pity for herself but from a deep shame that she could not speak of, not to anyone. She rolled over in her bed. She wrapped her arms around a pillow. She felt something. What?

She pulled it out. It was a bag of jelly beans.

What the hell?

Some four thousand kilometers away in Toronto, a man ran out of a conference room into a bathroom, and finally into a stall. He sank onto the floor, leaned against the wall, and then repeated the same name, "Sean." Moments before, he was leading a discussion in the conference room, when the same strange scene that appeared to Diana, appeared to him. However, the *perspective* was different. He saw the truck coming towards the two boys. He knew what would happen next. He sank into his chair, stunned and terrified. He couldn't speak. He started to fall out of his chair, then got to his feet and managed to make it out of the room, before sprinting to the only place he knew he could be alone.

He stumbled from the stall to the bathroom mirror. He thought he looked pale. His dark blonde hair was so slick with sweat that it had matted to his face. "I look struck," he thought. "As though I've seen a ghost." At six feet and one hundred and ninety pounds, he wasn't a small man, but he looked somehow weak and vulnerable in the mirror. He didn't want to face anyone like this. He tried to gather himself so he could return to the world waiting for him. He washed his face, tidied his hair, and straightened his clothes. When he touched his pants, though, he felt a lump in his pocket. He reached in and pulled out a bag of jellybeans. "Where did these come from?"

"I was that man in the bathroom. After I relived the most terrible scene of my life in that boardroom, I knew I was in a crisis. I could feel my reality tearing apart again. You can choose your metaphor. Maybe I was obscured in a vast forest. Or, the gods hated me. I was the loser, down and out."

I shifted in my seat. I was restless, but I couldn't figure why.

He paused.

"Would you like me to continue?"

I paused.

"Okay."

"I suppose I should have warned you that this story does contain trauma, grief and loss. But there is more. If you do want to stop, now is a good time to do so. I wouldn't blame you. I could leave you with this incident, and you could fill in the gaps. You would have a mystery that your mind could play with in bed."

"No. Please continue."

"Before I do, let's play some music?"

He nodded towards the jukebox behind us. It was a classic machine with haunting yellow and red lights.

"This was my gift to this place," he said. "I found it for sale at a flea market. I've always loved the Wurlitzer 1015, and I thought it would be an excellent addition. I like the way it glows. It's otherworldly. That ethereal light and the sound of music played on vinyl... It sends me. Anyway, I restored it and gave it to Sam, the owner, in exchange for the right to pick the music. He indulged me. He knew I was a bit of a nut for music. So, I guess he felt he could trust me."

We sipped our whiskey.

"I carried this story alone for a long time. As you can already tell, it's difficult. I should also say that I have found comfort while I lived this story on my own. In music. "A lonely man's best friend," as one writer aptly sang. I believe there is a song for every moment. And having the right music at the right moment can save us. Those things that tackle us, haunt us, separate us from each other, and burden us, are made lighter with words, melody, and rhythm. There is a song for everything we face. And that lets us know that we're not alone. That voice from your speaker, entering your room, it understands. I pride myself on finding the right tune for the right moment. And that can make all the difference. In other words, sometimes it's all we've got. So, I would like to offer you the same comfort I received. Like me, you are travelling this story alone with only a narrator. A little company might be nice for you."

He went over to the jukebox, pressed a few buttons and returned.

"I think you'll like these ones: 'Last Night' by Lightnin' Hopkins and one of the first recordings from that great soul from Ireland— 'T.B. Sheets'. Let's hear a bit before we move on."

I nodded, sat and listened.

"Northern Sky"
Nick Drake

"'We must inquire the way of strangers,' the great poet from southeastern Ontario wrote about going back home. When we leave behind those who loved us, who miss us, whose lives may not be as easy as our own, we must accept that we've deserted the tribe. We've left behind the glow of the shared fire to venture alone. And that, to some extent, is a rejection of them. If we approach them, we must do so as an outsider now. I think about this a lot. I'm from here. I feel attuned to the place, but I've been out of step with the culture. I left, and I've come back. Changed. But they put up with me—my strangeness. My neighbours recognize I do as little harm as possible, and I give what I can to others. For all of this to make sense, I need to take you back a little further. About forty years. To a time before I was born. In all of southeastern Ontario, the economy of farms and small businesses were passed on for generations. Space was vital, and everyone voted Conservative. We were children here. Our parents were too. Barely out of their teens when they had us."

He paused, and looked down into his half empty glass.

"Here, winters were proper winters. And summer was nearly as hot as summers could be. We lived our days between the stony ground and extreme fluctuations in weather. We sprang from generations of often frustrated people, surprised by joy, distrustful of ease, and in need of wonder. Our parents, their parents, grandparents, and usually at least a few generations more were from this area. This was true for Sean, Diana, and me.

Sean's mother, Doreen Hazelton, was a woman of devotion. As a child, her relationships were many and binding. These connections gave her security and meaning. By others, she was seen as dutiful, thoughtful, and kind. Her kindness was a broad pale light that shone on all that met her.

It was a warm glow, but impersonal. It shone on you because it shone at all times.

When she met the man that would be her husband — Kevin Ross — she loved how he was immediately drawn to her. Even at a young age, in high school, when his days were easy and so many around him seemed to be having fun, and while he was doing things that should bring him joy, a cloud hung over him. Doreen cut through the gloom. Consistently. And that constant light held him to her. She pulled him into her orbit, and he felt a shadow fall on him when they would part ways. That recurring feeling brought him back to her. To feel that warmth once more.

He would make sure he sat near her in the cafeteria at lunch. At parties, he would seek her out. He would rarely say much, but basked in her presence. Doreen, for her part, could sense the impact that she had on him. Very few of the boys at school seemed to appreciate her, but he did."

—

When Kevin saw her at a party at Joe Scott's house, he decided he would do something to win her. He stepped outside and reappeared about thirty minutes later. He breathed deep and walked briskly to her on the couch.

Be cool, man.

"Hey, Doreen."

"Hi!"

"Great party."

"Yeah..."

Just say it!

He gritted his teeth.

"Wanna see something cool?"

"Sure."

"Ok. We just gotta go outside."

They put on their shoes, and Kevin grabbed their coats.

Doreen was intrigued by Kevin. He was handsome, tall and had a vaguely olive complexion. She liked that.

I like catching you watching me. If you were someone else, it might be a little creepy. But with you... there's so much... care in your gaze.

"It's just down here. By the lake."

Doreen saw the light first and then the bonfire.

How sweet! Did he build this just for me?

Kevin finally felt at ease enough to look directly at her face.

I could stare at the glow of you for hours... and you would think I'm a weirdo.

"It's beautiful. I love bonfires," she offered.

"Me too... I've got a surprise for you. I need you to close your eyes, okay?"

Doreen covered her eyes with her hands while Keven threw an old piece of copper piping and a short length of garden hose tied together with a bit of twine into the fire.

"Okay, five, four, three, two, one. Open your eyes!"

Doreen dropped her hands to see fringes of green dancing at the top of the blaze's orange. The colour slid down to the base of the fire and then made great green flames, then blue ones, purple and then red. The fire was like a burning rainbow.

"Oh my god, Kevin!"

Kevin didn't watch the fire, but swelled with joy and pride at the wonder and happiness on Doreen's face.

"How did you do that?"

He paused. The ingredients seemed so ordinary that it would ruin the moment.

He leaned in and whispered in her ear, "I'll never tell you."

He held her face in his hands and kissed her gently. She sighed, and they kissed deeply.

Then she stopped, stepped back, and looked at Kevin.

"I've never felt magic as crazy as this," she whispered before kissing Kevin again.

—

From that night onward, at the age of sixteen, the two were inseparable. Doreen's confidence grew with Kevin's consistent affection, and Kevin felt lighter, more at ease because of it. She loved this relationship and could only imagine a life with them at the centre of it. So, two years later, at the end of high school, they married. It was 1970. He helped his uncle at his landscaping business, and she landed a job as a secretary at the local insurance company.

They were happy to move into a small apartment together in downtown Trenton. They loved setting up a house, having some money, and weekends together. He would often meet her for lunch and drive her to and from the insurance office each day. They lived in a glow of mutual satisfaction and innocence.

Doreen soon became pregnant with their first child, and their relationship began to shift. Her devotion moved to the child. Kevin was moving into the shadows. He sensed it coming during her pregnancy. It made him feel foolish for being jealous of a child that had not arrived, and it also scared him. He knew that he was losing her, and he needed all of her to keep him from the shadows on the edge of his life.

At night, Doreen was often tired from her pregnancy's demands and would go to bed early, without him. She knew that the child had wedged between them and that Kevin would need to chart his own course as a father. The demands of motherhood were pressed upon her. She didn't really have much choice in the matter. Fatherhood seemed like the opposite—a choice. You needed to choose it or deny it. It would just take time for Kevin to move into this role, she told herself.

The days became foggy after their daughter was born. They loved her, and named her Anna after her grandmother. In those early days, they were visibly moved and amazed to hear the girl coo. The three of them would lay together while Doreen nursed the child. She felt calm and satisfied, like hearing an old song she loved on the radio. One of those old big band jazz numbers her grandparents would play at their house. A waltz. It felt both familiar and like a distant, warm memory that she wanted to embrace. She sensed a similar peace in her husband.

Kevin felt a broader light around him. It was that of a young family. He was loved, he was needed, and that sustained him.

So, they had more kids. There was a calm in the rhythm of their lives that felt like twilight when the birds' chattering faded. She enjoyed it. She felt silence and peace fill them. Both submitted to it.

When her second child, Sean, arrived, their apartment grew smaller. So, she found a place in the nearby village of Scott's Mills for them to rent. It was one half of a duplex on a quiet, little dead-end street named Cambridge Avenue. The Trent River flowed behind their house. There were three bedrooms, and the small road was home to other young families.

By the time Alicia was born, Doreen's energies were nearly wholly devoted to the children. She had left her job to be at home. Kevin, on the other hand, felt lost in this world of growing children. The children looked to her for everything, and she gave them all she had. She had little left for him. And he seemed to have only a minor role to play. He was at a loss as to what to do about that.

His work, up until that point, had been tolerable, but nothing more. He was scrambling for a solution.

Other guys get married and have children but don't give much to their families. They just work and do stuff outside the home. Have I been a fool not to do the same?

Kevin began to work more and more, and would come home later more frequently. Those later arrivals included a strong scent of alcohol. There were heated arguments and chilling silences with Doreen.

After one of their disagreements, she made a decision.

I don't want to sit at home waiting for him with the children, and I don't want to rely on him for money. That means I'm going back to work.

When she went back to the insurance company, the two eldest had started school, and the youngest was at daycare. Kevin slowed down.

What the hell am I supposed to do now? Both of us are working. The kids are away. We don't really need the money.

He worked fewer days until finally, he was at home most days developing his new hobby: drinking.

"Our Prayer/Gee"
Brian Wilson

"We were the children of the poor. As children, we were oblivious to our vulnerable position. Instead, we played, unaware of our chains. The earth, sunlight, water, and space were our most common toys. Our relationships were as clear and pure as the water from a spring. We knew, even at our young ages, our greatest gifts were each other.

Before I entered kindergarten, my family moved to Scott's Mills, across the road from Doreen, Kevin, Anna, Sean and Alicia.

It was mid-June of 1978. Anna and my sister, Rachel, were almost eight. Sean and I were in our sixth year. The two girls could have passed for sisters with their blonde hair and fair skin. I was clearly a little brother. Sean had a slightly darker complexion and eyes.

Anna ran out of her home. She rarely walked anywhere. None of us did. It seemed like there was always a game to play or something to do in the neighbourhood. Especially on a Saturday or the last weekend before the end of the school year. One afternoon, after the cartoons were watched, Anna left her bowl of Lucky Charms with its pastel milk on the living room table, threw on her shoes, and went out to the street."

—

As she opened the door, she hollered to her little brother: "Sean, c'mon outside! I'm going!"

Rachel was already outside. A fresh pile of gravel had been left at the end of their street, just two houses down. Since it was a dead-end street, there was a gravel area for cars to turn around at the end of the road. Municipal staff would arrive with equipment to knock down this new pile of gravel and spread it over the turnaround on Monday. But for now, it

23

was something new on the street. Rachel was picking through the stones for colourful moments.

She and Anna were the eldest, so they both carried the warmth of being the sole receiver of their parents' love and affection for some time and adopted the sense of responsibility for their younger siblings. Sean, Alicia and I lived beneath the wing of their care.

We gathered around the pile of gravel. Sean and I climbed to the top. The girls chatted and continued to mine it for beauty. Within a few minutes, they had given up the search as the gravel was almost uniformly grey, and were now making plans to ride their bikes.

"Let's ride up to the witch's house," said Anna.

Rachel paused. She wasn't quick to take chances like this. But she also wanted to be agreeable. "Okay," she said.

Sean and I looked at each other, nervously. A glance that said it was terrifying but exciting. Plus, our older sisters would be with us. We were old enough to have fear. We knew there was harm out there. Lurking. It was no longer a feeling of separation from our loved ones. It moved into firm nouns like "monsters" or "murderers". And like all children, we found it more satisfying to find a subject for our fears than to receive abstract explanations. So, we had decided that the rarely seen woman who lived alone on the edge of Scott's Mills had to be a witch.

The girls rode ahead as we walked behind them. We were too young to have our own bikes. Sean and I each grabbed a handful of gravel. With signs, bottles, and cans on the ground, we would aim and have target practice along the way.

We looked at each other and smiled as we simultaneously struck a glass Crown Royal bottle on the side of the street. "Cool!" Sean exclaimed.

"We're the best!" I declared.

Sean laughed and started sprinting, looking over his shoulder to ensure I was following him.

I took up the challenge and caught up with him.

"The winners!" I exclaimed as I reached Sean and raised my friend's hand in the air in victory, alongside my own.

The girls had stopped up ahead of us by the grey and rotting fence of the witch's house.

None of us knew the name of the woman who lived alone in the house. We rarely saw her. Her wood-frame house was a more significant character to us with its peeling paint and an overgrown yard strewn with garbage. It created a dark and frightening scene. We all stood in silence in front of the house.

"I dare you to knock on her door," Rachel said, looking at me.

I was both excited and terrified by the challenge. I didn't want anyone to see the fear, though. So, I forced a smile.

"I'm not afraid."

"Then do it," she said.

There was a long pause.

Sean stepped towards the gate and looked back at me. He whispered our credo: "Heroes and villains."

As he began to open it, it creaked loudly and scared all of us.

The girls both let out a scream.
"AHHHHHHH!!!"

Anna and Rachel, still astride their bikes, quickly mounted them and rode away still screaming.

Sean and I also screamed.

We sprinted behind the girls until we were halfway home. Bikes strewn on the ground, we bent over gasping for air in a circle. We looked at each other and began to laugh.

"Even her gate is haunted," Anna said.

"We're crazy!" Rachel declared.

"Do you think it really was haunted and that it was screaming at us not to go in there?" I asked with great sincerity.

The girls laughed, and Sean pushed me a little.

"C'mon, let's see if we can go swimming today," said Sean.

"Good idea," I replied.

The girls nodded, and we ambled back to our homes.

"Bachianas Brasileiras No. 5"
Heitor Villa-Lobos

It was the last day of school: Friday, June 23, 1978.

The day was infused with the joyful anticipation of summer vacation.

In his excitement, Sean had woken early and bounded down the stairs for his breakfast. He gulped down a bowl of Cheerios and a small glass of orange juice, got on his right shoe, and was hopping on his right foot and trying to put on his left shoe as he went out the door. He sprinted across the road, not looking either way. He climbed the steps two at a time to the front door of my house, threw it open, and ran in.

I was eating cereal at the breakfast table with my sister, still sleepy. I wasn't surprised to see Sean. He often came over to my house in the morning to get me so we could go to school together. We knew that if we got out the door before Anna, we could grab her bike and ride it together to school. Our parents forbade us from doing this, but we loved it and tried to get the bike whenever we could manage it. Anna didn't seem to mind us taking it.

"Hi Sean," I said quietly.

"Hey, Sean," Rachel said, glancing over quickly. "Last day of school..."

"Yep."

Then Sean sent me a look that said, hurry up, let's go.

I quickly gulped down the cereal, walked the bowl over to the counter, and left it there while Sean started making his way out the door. I put on my shoes, ran down the stairs and across the road.

Sean was waiting with the bike and gestured for me to climb on the back of the seat. I hopped on, and we were off. We knew the first thirty seconds mattered the most. We needed to get out of the cul-de-sac and out of the sight of parents and sisters. Sean was a little older than me and a little taller, so he peddled for us. But he couldn't reach the pedals at their lowest point, so he would push hard when a pedal reached its peak and then let the momentum bring the other pedal upwards and then begin the process again.

We raced to the little trail at the end of the cul-de-sac that led to the garage's parking lot and the main road. We were free. We made it.

I looked over my shoulder as I reached the road, "We did it!"

"Yeah!" Sean agreed.

We continued to school along the main road that was busy with early morning traffic and then cut through the residential streets that led to the school.

"I'm going up to my Nana's cottage this weekend," said Sean. "Maybe you can come with me?"

"Okay, yeah, I'll ask when we get home."

"Let's stop at the drugstore," Sean said.

"I don't have any money."

"It's okay, I've got almost a dollar. I can buy us some stuff."

We scrambled off the bike, dropped it on the street and went inside the store. We bought one bag of barbecue chips and a bag of cinnamon hearts to share between us.

"Thanks, Sean."

"No problem."

"How about I push the bike, and you can eat?" I offered.

"Okay."

We slowly made our way, with the other children, to our last day of school. Summer was near; I could feel it. So was something else. I didn't know what it was. It left me feeling as though this moment was like the last instant of a dream, and soon I would be awake.

The school day started like any other, but there was an expectation of summer in the air. The energy was high, and people were happy. Even Mr. Fleming, the famously grumpy principal, was caught smiling several times that day. Including when our kindergarten class appeared in the gymnasium for our graduation.

All twenty-seven children from our kindergarten class were filed into the gymnasium, where we received our black gowns and hats. Sean and I looked at each other and laughed as teachers and volunteers handed out the black cloaks. Parents and other relatives sat in chairs, watching each child come forward to receive their diploma as a graduate of Scott's Mills Public School's kindergarten class.

Neither my family nor Sean's were there that day. My parents were working. So was Sean's mom. His father was at home. He was often at home and seemed in a bad mood, so Sean avoided him and didn't tell him about the ceremony.

After we collected the diplomas, our teacher spoke to the group.

"All right, you graduates, let's celebrate! One, two, three!"

At three, all twenty-seven of us threw our hats in the air and began clapping, yelling, and laughing. The crowd followed suit, laughing and clapping for us. Like water over a broken dam, we poured off the stage to our family members. Sean and I stayed behind and beside each other. We watched the other families for a moment. There were a few other children without parents there, but we stuck with each other.

It was lunchtime and we were expected to go home. There were a few snacks there though. We sped past the sandwiches to a large bowl of jelly beans, filled a small plastic bag that had been beside the bowl with them and ran out of the gym. We would eat lunch at Sean's house and play there. Kevin, Sean's father, was supposed to watch us.

"How about after lunch we see if we can sneak into Melissa's pool?" I asked.

"Cool."

We made our way outside to the bike rack at the school. Again, I sat on the back after Sean had hopped on the front. We kicked off and were on our way. Our journey would bring us past the one destination we couldn't avoid — the Bank of Montreal. We couldn't avoid it because it stood on the corner before the bridge and the only road that would take us home. And my mother worked at the bank.

She had told me numerous times that I wasn't allowed to ride the bike with Sean. It was too big for us. We had a plan we enacted each time we had to go by the bank. Just before we reached it, I would hop off the bike, and Sean would usually ride beside me until we were out of sight. In the morning, we left for school before my mother went to work, so we didn't have to worry about it for the first half of our journey.

I was peering into the building to see my mother, but I couldn't find her. So, I continued on with Sean, walking beside him. We crossed at the lights and began chattering away about our summer plans as we started across the bridge.

"I'm going to be an awesome diver this summer," said Sean. "I'm going to practice every day."

"I'm gonna stay the king of the cannonballs," I shouted to the sky.

We laughed.

I looked down at the bag of jellybeans to fish an orange one out for myself.

When Sean laughed, he swerved the bicycle a little, and as he swerved onto the road, he was struck and knocked down by a pick-up truck.

"Dark Was the Night, Cold Was the Ground"
Blind Willie Johnson

You're driving a truck in 1978. Your name is Diana. You're eighteen. You're in a rush. You hate the song on the radio, so you switch stations.

You don't know why the boy on the bike swerved, but he did. You barely even had time to process it. Then there was that terrible sound. It was a smack, a crunch, and a child's scream.

You brake hard, and the truck screeches to a stop. You first see me on the sidewalk. I'm stunned. I'm staring at something on the road. It is obviously Sean. I start running towards him. You quickly get out of the vehicle. You forget to take off your seat belt. You swear and fumble with it.

You scream when you see the scene.

"Oh my god! Oh my god! No!"

I'm holding Sean in my lap and speaking to him. I'm trying to comfort my friend. "It's ok, Sean. It's ok."

Sean is still conscious and trying to get up, and I'm trying to help him. He is bleeding from his mouth and nose, and his legs aren't working, so he is trying to pull himself up with his arms. He collapses. He falls unconscious and continues bleeding. Sean's colour is changing, his breathing is laboured and shallow. I'm holding him. You're in shock watching this.

I finally speak to you. "I'm going to get his dad. I'll go and get his dad!" I stammer.

You stay with Sean. You hold him. He is shivering in his fitful sleep. There is blood still falling from his mouth. You

32

finally break into action. You take off your sweatshirt, place it under his head and run to the nearest house for blankets.

You open the screen door and scream. "Please help! There's been an accident! I need blankets!" An elderly woman comes to the door, shocked.

"Blankets, I need blankets!" you scream. The woman moves as quickly as she can to her couch and fetches an afghan.

You grab it from her hand, and as you run out the door, you holler, "Call an ambulance!"

As you go back to the street, you see that cars have begun to stop at the site, and people are kneeling and standing by Sean on the pavement.

You instinctively push through the crowd and hold Sean in your arms. His body is still twitching and bleeding, and he still seems to be asleep. All you can do is wait. You look to the others near you with a pleading expression and back to Sean. "It's okay, it's okay." You hear the ambulance siren and the police siren.

Someone lifts you up from Sean's side, and two paramedics move in to get him. You close your eyes, and in agony, cry.

Piano Sonata No. 14 in C♯ minor *"Quasi una fantasia"*, Op. 27, No. 2, I. Adagio sostenuto
Ludwig Van Beethoven

He paused and looked around the bar. Blind Willie Johnson's moans and guitar picking trailed off...

"I don't know how to describe those last moments with my first best friend. All I can say is that I knew he was hurt and I wanted to help him. And I couldn't. And then he — as I knew him — was gone. He wasn't erased from existence. He had left his body and moved into another way of being. That was, and remains, what I understood happened to my friend that day.

The stark reality was present, as well: I was a co-conspirator of a purloined bike that led to an accident in which my partner-in-crime was struck by a vehicle, and it ended his time in this place. I was then a witness to his passing.

Sean's soul was slipping from him. I could see it. I had never thought of this sort of thing as a boy of only six. But I witnessed it that day. Even at our young age, we had a sense of a shared place where we all operated. And some of us have an understanding, hope, fear, or belief in another world or order beyond this one. For Sean, who he was beneath his graduation robes, was disappearing into this other world. It was a goodbye, not an ending. I knew that. He was going somewhere, but I couldn't go with him. I could nearly see it, and it was as though my soul had eyes of its own and caught sight of this place. His body was no longer his, but he, Sean himself, the essence of him, was still near us.

Then, and in a phrase: A great shudder moved through Diana and me. To shudder, as you know, is to feel your body shake out of fear or revulsion. It happens to you. You don't choose to do it. It chooses you; it's involuntary. We have no control over it. There's no other feeling or reaction quite like it. It comes from an emotion or a thought that causes the physical sensation.

My throat closed, a metal taste surfaced, and my urge to turn away was overcome by a need to help my friend. Then all of me, seen and unseen, shuddered. A deep rolling wave overtook me, and I was terrified, shocked, and felt the first pangs of loss. It didn't stop there.

Like a shudder, an earthquake is the result of energy erupting. This wave of energy shakes and sometimes splits open the surface. This break often occurs at fault lines.

The whole world around us experienced a seismic shift. Not just in the ground beneath our feet. It was a realityquake, I suppose. In our little part of the world, and in the young lives of us three, the surface of what was known suddenly rumbled, and rips appeared in it.

As I looked around me, everything—the truck, the bridge, the towering, swaying trees, the air, and us—shook and faltered with the blow, and it was as though a substance had been poured into them. A clear unknown form somewhere between sunlight and liquid formed a wave that moved through everything. I could feel it and see it in all the world around me: not just the people and objects but the air itself. And this substance made everything glow.

I have been able to see that low shining from that day onward when I allow myself. It's both a warm light and a sense of motion in all the things around me. It's as though love took on form. At times, the power of it overwhelms me."

He grew silent.

"I just need a moment." He looked out the window. Moisture gathered in the corners of his eyes.

He sighed. So deeply that it seemed to overcome him. It came from a deep recess. I watched his chest rise and fall. Rise and fall and let out a sound that seemed to carry a wealth of feeling in it. It was as though this act, its sound, and this man held in one moment a deep sadness, love, hope and gratitude all at the same time.

As he exhaled, he looked back at me. His cheeks were wet. So were mine.

"It's still a lot to bear. All of it. Sometimes...

That moment when our world was shaken, and my young friend was taken from us, caused an eruption. I don't know how far it extended. And yes, it changed my worldview. And to this day, I still, at times, feel the tremors from the incident. I suppose I always will.

And I think about Sean a lot, as you could imagine. From that moment, everything changed. To others, we were the people from the accident and the family of the boy who died. What no one knew is that moment also set two of us on new courses in life. We had to come to terms with not just Sean's death and our roles in it, but the knowledge of this eruption of otherworldliness into our very real world. This energy released into our lives could not be denied.

One notion was certain: who we were before the accident would not survive it."

"Corpus Christi Carol"
Jeff Buckley

I had to pull myself away from the experience and deal with the implications of it. I ran from the bridge, down the sidewalk and through the gas station parking lot for the trail. I wanted to move quickly. I tried to push myself faster and faster.

I pulled open the screen door of Sean's house and immediately saw his father sitting in a chair watching *The Price Is Right*.

"There was an accident! There was an accident!"

I ran to Kevin and pulled on the man's hand.

"What the hell happened?" he yelled.

I gasped for air. "Sean's been hit by a truck! On the bridge!"

Kevin ran out the door, barefoot, in a t-shirt and cut-off jean shorts.

I followed him out the door and ran behind him.

Kevin was going the long way, on the street.

"No, no, this way!" I said as I ran for the trail by the garage.

Kevin looked at me and changed direction. As he did, he yelled, "Go home! Go home now!"

I froze.

I watched as Kevin made his way on the trail, and as he moved out of sight, I ran behind him.

Police cars and other vehicles had stopped. There was a crowd on the bridge.

I slowed down. I didn't want to be in the middle of the crowd. Maybe my mother was there? I tried to peer through the people to see Sean, but I couldn't spot him. I could hear voices. "It doesn't look good." There was crying.

No one in my family knew I was there. No one would know that I was with Sean that day.

I ran away, and I kept running. For years.

"Mona Ki Ngi Xica"
Bonga

Just after 11:00 a.m., Anna would hear the kindergarten class cheering the conclusion of their graduation ceremony. She smiled in her seat, thinking of Sean. And it was a Friday, the last day of school. She imagined her dad would barbecue tonight. They would have hot dogs and then they would be given money to go to the corner store to get candy after dinner. She would go for Black Cherry ice cream or maybe a Fun Dip. She was on the cusp of the summer holidays. Weeks and weeks of lazy days spread out before her, where her world would be filled with play. Her body slackened just thinking about it.

As the day moved on, she knew something was wrong. It was like a weather front approaching. She looked out the window of her classroom for dark clouds on the horizon. She couldn't see them, but she could sense them. At lunch, she was sitting with her friends, just about to put another mouthful of her bologna, on white bread with Miracle Whip, in her mouth when she shuddered. It was like a great tide of misfortune overwhelmed her. So much so that that sandwich spilled from her mouth. Kids laughed.

"Shut up. I know."

The school day wasn't over, but she had been called to the office. Her aunt Karen, her mother's sister, and her husband Billy were waiting for her.

"Honey, you need to come with us," she said softly, the sound of phlegm thick in her throat and nose.

Anna didn't want to speak. She followed them out of the school's office and remained silent in the car. She wanted to spend as much time as possible, not knowing.

Her aunt and uncle were quiet in the front, but her aunt would let out a hushed cry every few minutes.

When they arrived at the hospital in Trenton, she grew hopeful. Hospitals are where people went to get well. She knew that. Someone was here to get well.

"Lento, Cantabile, Semplice from Symphony No. 3"
Henryk Gorecki

"If I had got here when he did... if I could have held him... I could have saved him. I know I could have..." Doreen pleaded to unseen forces.

Kevin had watched them put Sean in the ambulance and then sprinted home to get his car. The hospital was not far from Doreen's office in Trenton. He had to get her, he thought. He had to bring her to Sean. He needed her there.

As he pulled her away from her desk, the questions began.

"What happened?"

"Sean was hit by a car."

"How?"

"I don't know."

"Is he ok?"

"I don't know."

"Where is he?"

"At the hospital."

"I need to go there!"

"Yes. That's why I'm here."

She kept asking him questions about the accident on the way to the hospital that grew more desperate with each weak answer from him. He didn't know the driver and the details of how it happened. Or Sean's injuries. Her final question struck him hardest.

"Why didn't you stay with him?"

He knew his answer was wrong. When he arrived at the scene, they were searching for life in his son. Maybe he had just passed out. They were working on him as they placed him on the stretcher and put him in the ambulance. They had closed the door and sped away while he stood watching.

At that moment, he knew he needed Doreen. He had a deep longing for her to be with him right now. He had to find her. So, he offered no reply to her pleading question.

Moments after Doreen and Kevin arrived, a police officer told them that Sean had died before he reached the hospital. He had actually passed away at the scene, but they tried to resuscitate him in the ambulance and hospital.

"No... No... You can't tell me that," said Kevin.

"You can't do anything!" She barked at Kevin without even thinking about it.

The words struck him like a blow. He was already shaky, but this made his torso feel heavy and his knees weak. He thought he had earned it, so he said nothing. *She was the boy's mother and had a right to be upset. He had the news longer than her.* Kevin merely raised his chin.

"Would you like to see him?" the officer asked.

She nodded sobbing.

How can this room be so quiet and white? Doreen thought to herself. The walls, the lights, the bedding. Sean himself had little colour. *Oh no. His small face, nearly as white as the sheets around him.* Doreen could feel her legs were giving out on her but she was determined to make it to her son.

"Where has he gone?" she whispered as she placed his cheeks in her hands, and dropped tears on to his face.

She sobbed and sobbed, turning her back to Kevin. It felt as though her chest had been cracked open, and someone was pummeling her internal organs. Doreen had never felt anything like it before. Angry, violent noises fell from her. Her legs finally failed her and sinking to the ground, she curled into a ball. After a minute, the pain subsided. She gathered herself but felt something was missing. She looked at her body and was shocked to see it was intact.

She began to stand. Hands reached to help her. She was surprised she could move. The pain was decreasing, but she just felt drained and still draining. What was leaving her, she wasn't sure. Weakened, she let Kevin lead her out of the hospital.

Doreen was so engulfed in misery, she didn't notice the unilluminated spot forming on her chest. During the drive home, she felt something strange there. She looked down to see that her blouse had a tiny hole between her breasts. And beneath it was a dark spot. As though someone poked a hole in her to reveal that beneath her skin was not tissues, fluids, and bone but a shadow

.

It appeared suddenly and began to grow, almost silently. It was a hole in her that emitted a low sound of rushing air that you could hear if you lay your head on her chest. A portion of her breastbone had no skin, no bone or any of the internal elements. If you were to look upon her bare chest, it would look like a gloomy space had formed on her body.

Why this occurred is purely a matter of science. As we've been told, a black hole is formed when a star dies. Its gravity fails, and all matter comes crashing down upon itself. Anything that enters is crushed by a great force.

One of the stars that formed Doreen had died. As this celestial body passed away, it turned in on itself. The light it once gave was now gone. And any object that dared to cross the black hole's horizon line was immediately crushed into emptiness.

She retreated to her bedroom, alone, and closed the door behind her. She fell upon her bed as though someone had knocked her to it or threw her on it. For days there was no reprieve. Her other children could bring her no joy. Her husband only made her angry. Fits of useless, pitiless anger that she was too disgusted with to recognize.

She wanted to touch the hole that first day in her bedroom. She noticed that it had grown to the size of a clementine.

She wept, and while she did, she moved the index finger of her right hand towards the spot on her chest. Curious, she slowly pushed the tip of her finger into it. It disappeared, and she suddenly felt a force crushing the end of it. She moaned and withdrew the digit to see that a quarter of an inch of it was gone. It had just disappeared. She looked at the end of her finger and was compelled and disgusted at the sight of layers of skin, the red, bleeding flesh and bone. She ran to the bathroom and got a bandage to cover it. The pain was excruciating.

It feels strange to feel something.

As she walked out of the bathroom, she saw the door to Sean's room was open. She stepped into it. The room had the faint smell of her son. She wanted more. She looked around. She found some of his clothes in a laundry hamper, pulled out one of his t-shirts and held it to her face.

It's like he's near. She felt something strange in her chest and saw that part of his shirt had fallen into the black hole and disappeared. She quickly pulled the shirt away.

She scolded the hole. "No!"

She then fell onto Sean's small bed, holding the shirt, weeping.

When she woke, she wasn't sure how long she had slept. For a moment, she didn't know where she was and had forgotten what had happened. Then it all fell on her. She sank back into the bed.

Anna came to the door. Doreen didn't want her to see her and tried to shoo her away.

"Go to your room, please," she said in the gentlest tone she could muster.

"Ok... What are you doing?"

Doreen had forgotten about the black hole.

"Nothing. Nothing. Please go to your room. Now."

Anna returned to her room quietly.

Doreen knew that she had to figure out how to live with the black space in her. A saucer would have been the right size to cover it, but too heavy. She needed something light and arced to sit above the hole and not be consumed by it. She looked around the room and saw the small Fisher-Price record player that had been Anna's before it was passed along to Sean. The surface on which the records would sit—the platter—was about the right size, and the centre portion dropped. The circle it created was just big enough to hover above the hole.

So, she went to work on the little red and white plastic record player. It was harder to take it apart than she expected, but she did so in the end with a butter knife from the kitchen.

She placed the edges of the platter beneath her bra on the two sides and the bottom. A piece of it slipped into the disturbance on her chest and disappeared. Otherwise, it worked well.

As she wore it, she thought of Sean's small hands on it and his favourite songs. Then she somehow felt protected and secure with this new development in her life and on her body. As a child, she had read about saints who underwent transformations. *Sean had died, and something strange happened to me in the hospital when I saw him. I've been invaded, plundered, and reconfigured. This oddity on me is the sign of it.*

But the constant low whistling of wind emitting from her chest terrified her. In the days that passed, she would sit with that sound. To be terrified was her punishment, and it was the only feeling greater than the loss of Sean. She made herself utter the words aloud: "The death of my son. At six." There were no more tears for now—just bitterness.

"Holland, 1945"
Neutral Milk Hotel

I didn't cry. For the rest of the day of the accident, I felt numb. Like I was a step behind myself and everything I did. I noticed there was blood on the bottom of my t-shirt. No one else saw the stain, or at least they didn't ask me about it. But I threw the garment away just in case they started to ask questions. My mom came home from work because she heard about the accident, learned that it was Sean, and recalled that I had planned to go to his house for the afternoon.

When I got home, she was there. On the phone with my father.

"No, I think he died," was the line that reverberated in my head.

She paid little mind to my presence. After she finished her call, she turned to me.

"Have you had lunch?"

I knew that I hadn't, but I had no appetite. I shook my head. I was afraid to speak. I was waiting to get in trouble. But no punishment came. She never talked about it to me that day or in the days and years to follow.

Anna would arrive home at the end of the school day and speak to my parents about it at dinner. She had heard about the collision at school.

Anna broached the subject at dinner. "Did you hear anything about an accident?"

There was a pause.

My mother answered with a clipped, "Yes."

"I heard Sean was hit by a car."

"He was."

"What happened?"

There was a pause before my father spoke. In the space of his hesitation, my mother broke into tears.

"He *was* hit by a car, honey."

"Is he okay?"

"No... he died."

"What, why?"

"He just got hurt too much to get better."

"I don't..." Anna fell into tears and my father wrapped an arm around her.

I stared down at my plate. I didn't want to be there; I didn't want to be seen. But I felt as though I could not contain the secret, the pain, the rage, and the shame. But I accomplished my goal. I managed not to say a word. I could now hold to it in silence with a strength that would be at least enough to carry on like this.

"Everybody Knows"
Leonard Cohen

Steve turned the corner onto Oxford Street in Scott's Mills and saw the small duplexes. His mind was racing.

These people don't have any money. These are just rentals. I've never been down this little street. These people would be so angry with my daughter for driving the truck. It was just a goddamn accident. It's not her fault. What does he want from me?

He steeled himself for a fight or to do whatever he needed to do to defend his daughter.

Steve had the appearance of a once handsome and athletic man who had quit sports but maintained the confidence and assertiveness that could turn to aggression with ease. He was just over six feet tall with dark hair greying now that he was in his forties.

He looked at the sheet of paper he got from the Police Department: "Kevin Ross. Father. Doreen Ross. Mother. 6 Oxford Street." The family name was familiar. He went to the front of the house, paused, and knocked on the screen door. Sean's father came to it. It was now after dinner, and only he and his wife were home. Doreen was in her bedroom alone. Kevin was sitting in his La-Z-Boy chair, staring out the window, drinking whiskey straight.

Kevin didn't open the door but stood on one side, looking out at this man. He didn't want to let anyone in.

"That was your boy today, I understand, that was in the accident."
"Yep." He glanced at the man's eyes.

"Well, I want you to hear it from me... we're terribly sorry about it."
"Why are you sorry?"

"Well," he said a little indignantly, "I'm Steve Glendon. It was my daughter that drove the truck." He cleared his throat.

"It was, was it?" Kevin was becoming defiant.

"Yeah, it was. Terrible thing." There was a pause.

"We wanted to let you know we're sorry. My daughter is a good kid. It was an accident. A terrible accident — but I'd like to cover all your funeral costs and so on. I just wanted you to know that — my daughter was supposed to go off to university, and I don't want this thing to be hanging over her. I don't think we need to ruin two lives in this."

Kevin went silent for a moment. His mind was speeding up. *Funeral. Funny. When I woke up this morning, I didn't think about death, and now I have to put up with this jerk in the doorway talking about my son as an expense. Everybody knows the deal is rotten. That's all there is to this.*

"Yeah, you pay." He turned from the door and headed back to his chair.

Steve walked back to his truck, a little confused and offended but decided to let it go.

He sniffed. "I'm no one's fool."

"Death Bell Blues"
RL Burnside

The coffin seems so big for Sean, Doreen thought.

I can't believe I've never been in here before. I've lived my whole life around here but have been able to avoid Thompson's Funeral Home. My god, does he ever talk a lot. The details, yes, the details, you will take care of all the details. It must be strange to go to work each day and deal with death and grieving. How does he do it? I gotta try to be patient.

"Yes, that one looks nice. Cherrywood is fine." *Almost cheerful. Is that ok? Is it wrong to bury your son in something with a bright colour?*

"It's fine."

What the hell does he know, saying to me "he is too big for an infant's coffin."

"Don't talk about my son and what he isn't to me."

I sound like an animal with these low cries and guttural noises. I don't care — the pain of it. The closest is childbirth. The only thing more painful than bearing a child is to lose one.

And then this goddamn thing in my chest.

Ok. I've gotta choose the size of the coffin, too. It's a special size. That's nice. Something like a treat for Sean. Not quite as large as a full adult casket. He's just a boy of six years old. But he has room in there. That's nice. I guess that's nice. He's not crammed into a small space. Goddammit.

"The average size for an adult was eighty-four inches long and twenty-eight inches wide. Sean's would be seventy-two inches long and the same width."

"Six feet." *I can do the math, even with this ringing in my head.*

"Six feet is all he gets now. A foot for every year."

Oh, Jesus, why can't I stop the crying. I can't do this anymore.

With that, Doreen got to her feet and left the funeral home and began to walk home. Her sister, Karen, had driven her, but Doreen didn't want to wait for her.

Karen finished the funeral arrangements and picked up Doreen about an hour later. She had walked nearly halfway to Scott's Mills. Karen expected that and found her on Highway 33.

At the funeral itself, Doreen detested the prim, sanitized, and muted features of the ritual.

Nothing this poor minister or Karen can say will carry the weight of what happened or can uplift us. It feels like a dress rehearsal for one of our tedious high school plays. I don't want to be in this, and I don't want to watch this. I have no words for any of you. Let me close my eyes and be in the dark with my tears and sorrow.

"The Lord is close to the brokenhearted and saves those who are crushed in spirit."

Yes, that's right.

"There was a light in Sean's eyes that we all loved. We need to hold to that light."

Oh, Karen.

Doreen felt numb. It wasn't until they reached the grave, and she saw how the green grass fell into a dark pit where they would lay her boy, that she fell apart. Walking to it, she could faintly hear the whistling hole in her chest grow in volume. She fell as she reached the edge of it.

"Honey, honey, no... no, no..." was all she said.

Teetering on the edge of that dark hole, she struggled to let out a deep grief that sounded even worse than the whistling in her chest. She then lay on the side of that hole moaning and pushed away the hands of those who tried to help her to her feet.

Kevin couldn't go there. He did not walk with her to the side of the grave, and he did not go to her when she fell. He felt frozen. She was his light, and now that light was gone. He was lost. He tried to make sense of it all by creating the story of it in his mind.

It was the last day of school. Sean had worn one of those square hats and robes for graduation from kindergarten. I could have gone to the school ceremony and maybe taken him out for a burger and ice cream. But I didn't do it. It seemed like something only women would do or at least organize the thing. And now my boy is dead.

People slowly filed out of the cemetery. His brother, Marty, came to him as he stood by the grave.

"Man, can I drive you home?"

Kevin only shook his head.

"I'm sorry." He lit a cigarette.

Kevin scanned the crowd and saw Steve, who gave him a wave.

"Fuckin' wave at me." He grabbed his brother's cigarette, took a drag, and put it out on the lapel of his own suit.

Marty said nothing in return. He felt confused and stared for a few seconds at the black mark on his brother's chest. He handed Kevin a mickey of Crown Royal. Kevin sipped from it and then drank again. He then slipped it into a pocket of his suit.

People were filing out of the graveyard. He ignored them.

"I'll see you later, Marty," he finally said.

An hour or so passed. The night was growing. He sat beside the small grave marker and looked at the turned earth. His boy was in the ground. The hole was so small. Sean was so little.

"My boy, my boy," is all he could bring himself to say between deep swigs from the whiskey bottle.

"I won't leave you alone here tonight. I'll stay with you... I love you. I love you." He realized he hadn't uttered those words to Sean in over five years. The last time, Sean wouldn't have understood them. He was just a cooing baby.

He then just fell into tears and began to rub the dirt from the recently turned ground on to his face. Muddy rivulets ran down his face and onto his white shirt.

He lay on his back beside the grave.

"I'll lie with you, my boy. I'll lie with you."

He wept, and once the mickey was finished, he worked on the bottle he had brought with him and stored in his vehicle. The sun began to set, and night settled into the country graveyard. He watched the stars start to shine and slowly move above him. They seemed to do it so thoughtlessly. The moon appeared over the trees. It was a beautiful summer night, which only deepened his grief. He listened to the crickets, and as the night grew darker and the bottle grew lighter, he became drowsy.

He woke to hear a small voice whisper. "Dad."

It was Sean. He rushed to his father, and Kevin sat up quickly and held him. He wept tears of joy.

"Oh, my boy, my boy, stay with me here, my boy."

He rocked Sean in his arms and gripped him tightly. He had never felt so happy in his life as he did at this moment. He could feel his boy's small arms around him and his head on his chest. He pulled back to look at his son's face, and as he did, Sean whispered to him again.

"Goodbye."

"No! Sean! No, you need to stay here with me. From now on, you need to stay here with me. I'll take care of you from now on. I'll take better care of you from now on, but you have to stay here with me."

Before he could finish, Sean was gone.

Kevin sat in the cemetery until the sun rose.

Maybe, just maybe, he will come back.

But he didn't.

He gathered himself, brushing his hair with his hands and tucking in his shirt. He picked up the empty bottles he had left by the grave. He drove out of the cemetery and on to the road, nearly hitting an oncoming car because his eyes were fixed on his rearview mirror.

He was surprised when he got home to find a truck parked in front of the house. It looked brand new—a 1979 Chevy Silverado. Electric Blue.

"Who the fuck is here with that?" He had stopped for breakfast on the way, then slept in his truck for a while, so it was now nearing noon.

Maybe someone to share their sympathies.

He saw a note under the wiper blade on the driver's side as he walked by it. "Sorry for your troubles. I hope you enjoy the truck. Steve."

He opened the door to see the keys on the seat.

The damn guy couldn't even speak to me at my son's funeral, and now he gives me a truck. A truck. If Sean had been shot, would he have given me a gun? Asshole. It's all to protect his little girl, his precious little girl. He takes my son and just wants to protect his daughter.

"Screw that."

He opened the door of the truck but stopped and vomited in the vehicle's bed, wiped his face and climbed into the driver's seat.

"Rowboat"
Johnny Cash

"The goddamn party is a tradition!" Steve bellowed to his wife, Lillian. "And I'll be damned if I'm going to cancel it because of a car accident. Besides, it's too late. If you wanted to cancel it, we should have done so yesterday."

Lillian stared at him. I'm done with this, she thought to herself. She turned and walked from the room. She was an attractive woman in her forties with mid-length brown hair and brown eyes. She had a way about her that seemed to take exception to whatever was happening in her vicinity.

"If you're worried about Diana, I wouldn't—she won't leave her room anyway. That's all she does is sit in her room."

Lillian was already at the top of the stairs when he added that last line.

Steve followed her over. "I've got Buddy and his girlfriend to help me out. So, you can go and have your fit."

Lillian slammed the door.

Two hours later, the party was happening. It was a summer party that Steve liked to hold for his salesmen. Summer was their big season, and he wanted his team to feel appreciated so they would work all of the long hours needed to make the revenue targets.

About twenty people were gathered around his pool. Some were swimming. A few of the guys talked with Steve as he grilled steaks beside the pool.

Their house was a massive affair just outside of Trenton, set back from the road with a large, well-mown lawn. He had the home built to his specifications five years earlier.

If there hadn't been a series of shrubs along the pool area, Steve and his guests would have likely noticed a truck sitting along the edge of the road, in front of the house.

What's with all the cars? Is the fuckin' guy havin' a party? He's havin' a fuckin' party! The day after my son's funeral. That goddamn cockroach.

Kevin took a swig from a bottle of whiskey in his lap, then turned the truck's wheel and hit the gas.

Son of a bitch. He was driving over the front lawn. Gaining speed.

Prick.

He turned the wheel hard, hit the gas pedal, and the back end of the truck shot pieces of the lawn into the air. He continued making circles and punching the gas, leaving a torn trail in his wake.

From her lounge chair, Steve's assistant, Gloria, caught sight of the truck through a break in the cedars. She sat up with her piña colada in-hand. "Hey, Steve! Someone's out there, tearing up your lawn."

Steve and the other guys looked to her in her bikini, out to where she was motioning, back to her in her bikini, and finally back to the truck that was still ripping up the lawn.

Steve ran from the grill towards the truck. *What in the hell? Who is that?*

As he ran down the hill, Kevin caught sight of him and raised the bottle of Crown Royal out the window.

"Cheers, asshole!"

He drove past Steve, brandishing the large spatula he had been using on the barbecue, up the hill and reached a gate to the pool.

"Get the fuck off my lawn!"

The guests were gathered outside the pool area. Watching.

Kevin backed up the Chevy and lined it up to get a good angle at the gate. Then rolled up the window.

Steve was now running back to the pool. As he neared the truck, Kevin began moving forward slowly. The truck was too wide for the entrance and struck the posts of the gate instead.

"What the hell are you doing?!"

Kevin backed up about ten feet, hit the gas and went through the gate, knocking down the poles. He slowed as he reached the pool then gave the Chevy one last push on the gas, and the vehicle dove into the pool.

He and the truck quickly sank to the bottom. Water poured into the cab around his ankles.

He took another belt of whiskey.

It's like they dug a hole in the bottom of my soul.

The liquid reached Kevin's knees, then waist—and then he felt someone grabbing his shirt through the window. He looked to see a man there. Kevin swung at him and clumsily punched the stranger in the shoulder.

I'm going down with the ship. I wanna go under. I'm just gonna close my eyes. Hands again. I don't wanna fight anymore. Fine.

He felt himself being pulled out of the car, pushed the hands away, and swam to the surface. People lined the edge of the water, but Kevin pulled himself up at the side of the pool ignoring them all. He began to walk through the crowd when Steve grabbed his arm. "I'm gonna kill you!"

"I think your family has killed enough of my family. But I would love it if you gave me a chance to take a run at you."

He punched Steve in the face, and he immediately fell to the ground.

"Get up. Get up!" Kevin hollered.

The onlookers grabbed Kevin.

Steve looked up at him. He'd seen that look before in men. There was nothing left for him to lose, no leverage for reasonable negotiation. "Let him go."

Kevin walked out of the pool area without a word and kept walking.

"Blue Moon Revisited"
Cowboy Junkies

For Anna, the days that followed the accident were strange and hazy ones. It was the start of the summer holidays, so she expected to be home, but she had assumed her time would be more joyful, of course. Instead, her parents often disappeared from the house, and when they were there, they were not themselves. They were only a fleeting physical presence. They became their absence.

Her aunt and uncle played a more significant role. They made meals and took care of her and her sister.

She was left with her thoughts, and they first turned to the bicycle. She would think about it for decades. It was an object of desire, then great pleasure, and finally her greatest grief. It's funny, she thought, how she coveted the machine and now despised it.

She was six when she began to want a bicycle. She had seen older classmates ride to school and loved to watch their effortless glide on their bikes. Plus, many were of cheerful colours she only ever had in the details of her shirt or dress or on her socks — sunny yellows, searing reds, and electric blues.

But mostly, she loved the feeling she got from riding the bicycle. It was like she was flying. Or, at least what she imagined flying must feel like. The world around her became fantastic — the sidewalk and streets blurred, the excitement of travelling fast made the colours of the houses and cars brighter and more spectacular. Her brain had to move quickly to process all that was happening. But now, it was gone. Partially destroyed, she presumed, by the accident. She never asked about it and didn't want to lay her eyes upon it again.

On the day of the accident, Sean had asked her to ride it. He often did. She repeatedly refused because riding the bike gave her such great pleasure, and she wanted to ride it herself, to and from school. But it was the last day of school, and Sean was going to graduate from Kindergarten. Their mother had dressed him in a button-down shirt and nice pants.

She loved her little brother and wanted to do this for him. At nine, she had already developed a deep sense of generosity, and it extended to those she held affection. And Sean ranked among those she loved the most.

So, her final moments with him involved granting him access to her bright yellow Schwinn Mini Scrambler.

The night before the funeral, Anna lay in bed, staring into the dark with these thoughts. On her way from the bathroom, after she brushed her teeth, she passed Sean's room. The door was still open. Her mother was gone. It had been left untouched since the accident. She paused in the doorway. She couldn't see much in the dark but the outline of furniture and some toys and clothes on the floor. She didn't want anyone to clean it.

She made her way to her room and lay on top of the sheets with no blanket on her in the warm June night. Her breathing felt difficult. She was tired. It was a new sort of exhaustion for her. She closed her eyes. Soon, Sean appeared to her. He was standing at the foot of the bed as though he had been waiting for her. He raised his arms until they were in front of him and cocked his head slightly.

"Sean," she said, "Sean, I'm here. I'm here. Come to me."

He didn't move, so she quickly crawled to him and felt his arms around her, and then he was gone. She felt a presence like those pockets of cool air on summer days that leave you surprised and unsure of what they are or where they come from... This time she wept when it arrived.

She couldn't sleep, and it was now the day of the funeral. She quietly left her bedroom, crept down the stairs, and quietly opened the front door. It was just before five, and her family and the rest of the village were asleep. It was a strange time, not night, but it wasn't quite morning.

A thick summer fog hung in the air.

I love this fog. Everything looks different. I feel lost in it.

She wandered in this mist towards the river. It didn't take long. The river was very close to their home. Her parents joked that when they rented the house, it came with a pool — the Trent River. The current was moving swiftly as it was just the start of summer.

She could hear her mother warning her to stay away from the river. But it was beautiful this morning. She was suddenly stopped in her tracks.

The fog was somersaulting through the air above the water. Birds were beginning to sing. They swung slowly in the heavy air. The dark sky was being broken by a light in the east. It illuminated the scene but was too weak to burn off the haze that cloaked the moment. She closed her eyes, and it almost felt like arms around her.

I wish they were around me.

Anna was lulled by the scene and a presence that was overcoming her. She was lifted from the ground by unseen hands. The sun shone brightly into her. She closed her eyes to the dazzle and quickly fell into sleep. She woke and wasn't sure how much time had passed. The sun had risen.

She felt bigger, more powerful but also tired. It was a deep fatigue that would stay with her. It was like a hunger she didn't know how to sate.

If you were to look upon Anna, you would see a new person. She was an adult now. Not only was she five feet and four inches tall, but the so-called baby fat of childhood had dropped from her face, allowing her cheekbones to stand out, her chin to become more prominent, and her eyes more piercing. She stayed at this height and looked like this for years to come.

When it ended, she sat on the river bank and watched the sun continue to rise in the east. She didn't understand what had happened, but she knew something of significance occurred. The light was burning off the dew, the village began to stir and cars were moving on nearby streets. A door opened and closed—a muffled voice.

She knew she couldn't avoid the world, so, after a few minutes, she made her way home. As she walked, she took strides, looked around, and tried to accustom herself to her new body.

More changes were to come to Anna. After the funeral, her father continued disappearing for days at a time. When he was home, he was silent and smelled sickly sweet and acidic at the same time. He seemed dangerous. She avoided him. It was just two nights after the funeral that she came downstairs for a snack. The kitchen and the adjoining dining room were dark. She turned on the kitchen light.

"Turn off the goddamn light!" a voice bellowed from the dark.

She was surprised to find her father sitting on the couch. She had thought he was gone again to wherever he went. But he was home. There were no lights on, and the TV wasn't running. He sat in the dark with just a glass in front of him and an ashtray.

She said nothing, turned off the light, and continued to the fridge.

There was a palpable tension in the house after the funeral. She remembered going to her grandparents' house on the lake in the winter. On cold days when the ice was thick, they played on it while her father and grandfather would go fishing on the frozen water. It was a silent place, and then the ice would suddenly release a belt of thunder. It was the pressure of the ice. She knew what it was, but it still scared her every time. It wasn't just the noise but the sense that this seemingly safe surface could burst open at any moment. She knew the thunder was coming to her home, but she was surprised at her reaction to it.

Anna opened the fridge door, and the light from within shone through the room.

"What the hell do you think you're doing?"

She felt defiant. "I'm just getting some food. Hungry?"

"Hurry up and get out of here."

She said nothing.

"You're not so smart now, are you?"

She said nothing and kept her back to him.

"Naw, you thought you were pretty smart when Sean died, didn't you? Your mother told you not to let him use your bike, but you let him, didn't you? You let him do it, and then he died. There you go. You're so smart... you killed your brother." And then he laughed, a low cackling, menacing laugh.

She was devastated. She felt as though she was being punched repeatedly with each syllable he threw from his mouth. But a force rose in her. She didn't know from where, but she held herself up and even stiffened herself with outrage and growing power. She was disgusted by him. And it shocked her. She'd never felt disgusted by her own father.

She said nothing but just stared into the fridge. There was barely anything in it. A few dishes that people had brought them: brown wilted lettuce, a shriveled cucumber... and no milk.

That moment she decided she would not let him see her pain, confusion and, most importantly, guilt.

Did he really think he was telling her something she hadn't thought of already? Had she not thought over and over and over again, *what if I just had not let Sean take my bike?*

Anna knew her father had been withdrawn and that he was seething with sadness and anger. All of them were feeling it. Part of her couldn't admit to herself that she knew what was coming from him. But still, it angered her when it arrived.

She'd also gone through numerous scenarios in which she had the bike, and maybe because she was a little bit bigger, the accident could still happen, and she would get badly hurt but not die. She made a list in her head of the injuries she would be willing to sustain for her brother not to have died: broken legs, arms, life in a wheelchair, and even death. She knew if she were asked right now, she would trade places with Sean. Knowing that gave her a sort of relief.

I would give it all to keep him forever from harm.

She realized she couldn't hear her father anymore, but he was still hurling insults and accusations. She was numb, immune.

"We're out of milk. We have been for days now. I'll get it myself tomorrow, for chrissake."

Kevin fell silent.

From that day forward, she felt a purpose. There was an external change, but there was also an internal shift. She had quickly grown in height and lost the childish roundness in her face. Perhaps most noticeable were the crow's feet that landed on each side of her eyes. She was tall, slightly wrinkled, not just around her eyes but also her mouth and chest. She had the body of a thirty-year-old woman at the age of nine.

When she slammed the fridge door, she knew her childhood was over. If anyone in the family could see her, they would've noticed the stark, premature change from a child to a woman. And that woman had a purpose.

She had found her calling as a caregiver. She was the eldest sibling, Sean was gone, and there was just baby Alicia now. She would be the mother to her. She kept the little one close, and she tried to ensure she was always safe and happy and well-fed. As the days and weeks passed, Anna found that by bringing joy to her sister, she found a trickle of happiness in herself. It was as though she had excavated herself to discover that small vein of light and was able to deliver it to her sister and, in fact, had nourished them both.

As Anna grew older, she would maintain this role of the surrogate mother, bereft of parents. Their parents were now just landlords. So, it wasn't surprising that she would excel when she went to school in the fall and for the years to come. She would be diligent, responsible, and well-behaved.

"Something In The Way"
Nirvana

The facts of the accident played over and over in my young head: I was never supposed to be on the bike. I had to get off it, so my mom wouldn't see me. We walked a little bit, and then Sean was hit by a truck. And then he died. The pictures of it surfaced, and I would try to push them away. When I slept, they appeared again, and I had no way to stop them.

I would think: death was here, but I'm alive. It all seemed wrong. And now the world seemed wrong. Something was wrong with me. All of me was wrong. I was an abomination.

I just wanted to hide with my pain. I was drawn back to the site of the accident on the bridge. I was drawn to it the day after the crash. The pavement still had stains and small pieces of glass. I had to see it, and I had to look away.

I saw the small path that ran down the hill beside the bridge. I followed it. It was now summer, and the little creek that ran beneath the bridge was dry. The world down there was now just a dark place. I would run away to it. I could escape my parents' house and just sit alone in the dark, in the cool underneath the bridge.

It was just me and the other refuse of the world — graffiti, soda cans, wrappers. I felt discarded. I threw myself away. Shame was growing within me. It whispered to me in the dark: "If you hadn't got off the bike so your mother wouldn't see you, Sean wouldn't have died. It was your fault. Why should *you* live when he died?"

The shame insisted I carry it alone. So did the fear of reprisals for doing what I should not have done that day. Adults had discussed the accident with each other, there had been hushed conversations between my parents, but no one had talked to me about it since that day. I still hadn't been asked about it. I was waiting to get in trouble and hoping to be comforted, but neither happened. Somehow, no one had thought to ask about the boy who was there when Sean died. Sean's parents and his sister were deep within their own grief. I knew that. My parents couldn't seem to connect the pieces. And I wanted to hide it. I would be alone with this.

I had disobeyed the rules, and now Sean was gone. So, I agreed to carry this burden without the help of anyone. No one knew that I was there, that I was with Sean when he died. When I decided that I was on my own with this, I finally cried. I wept among the garbage and the wildflowers.

When I was done, I walked to where the creek met the broader Trent River. I placed an empty Dr. Pepper can I found on the shore into the water. Carefully, so that it wouldn't fill up with liquid and could possibly journey on. I took comfort in watching it float and travel. I loved watching the tiny object carried by currents that sprung from somewhere unknown. Those powers could take it away to places far from here. It was no longer garbage. It was no longer worthless. It was something greater than itself if it could navigate the waters.

Knowing that I couldn't avoid the world around me any longer, I would emerge from beneath the bridge, and trudge home to try and live among others.

My young mind could not comprehend what would happen next. I was to be changed. Alchemy was at work within me. I only knew what I saw, my responsibility, and that I had to carry this shame alone. And this was too much for anyone — let alone a six-year-old boy.

Unbeknownst to me, I was about to move from singular to plural. I was going to become two boys. There was me from June 22, 1978; the day before the accident. He was poised to become a memory. I would now be a by-product of the accident and its impact. And that changed me so much that for a long time, I became my reactions to it.

BRUCE SUDDS

.

On the third day after Sean's death, I clambered down the bank and stood in the half-light under the bridge. Suddenly, I could feel my body begin to shake. I could feel parts of myself growing or falling away. I slapped the concrete walls crumbling around me. I punched them as the chaos of this uncontrollable force overtook me.

"Sean!"

I kicked everything around me — the garbage, the frail plants that were able to find a meagre life here and the ground itself. Falling to my knees, I dug the palms of my hands into the dirt and screamed into the earth. My tears only muddied the soil. It made me think of the mud pies I would make with Sean beneath my front porch. I shoved the dirt into my mouth. I wailed until I fell flat on my stomach weeping. Overcome, I curled into a ball and fell asleep on my side.

I was in pieces — a portion of myself. I would answer to my name as it was called, but the person who answered wasn't fully me. I was reduced, stunted, and frail. That boy, the boy I was, we will refer to as Devin.

Then, there was the boy that was to be born from this death and its impact — my twin. I had been shattered into pieces, and as much as I tried to gather them up in the dark recess offered beneath the bridge, in my long walks or alone at night in my room, there was no way to gather them to form a whole. Instead, a new boy was created. Alexander.

'I' am no longer a part of this story.

"Stand By Me"
Ben E. King

The pieces of a new person that sprung from Devin lay on the ground. They were twitching limbs, a damp torso, and a sleeping head. The eyes were closed. A wind blew through the space, kicking up dirt. The pieces assembled while Devin slept on the rubble and refuse. The wind blew warmly around them and woke them both. They opened their eyes at the same time and squinted in the dusty wind.

Devin was startled by all of this. He knew something strange was afoot. He sat in the humid wind with this naked boy beside him. Was this boy Sean? Had Sean come back to him? Devin couldn't comprehend that this boy had been formed from him.

He looked to be about the same age. Devin was startled to see him. He didn't want to see anyone here. He stood up in shock. Wanting to run away but feeling he couldn't do so, he sat in tense silence. The naked boy said "Hello" as though a declaration. Devin managed a weak, "Hi."

Something had changed. He felt an odd presence. Maybe Sean was with him as a spirit now, and this was the ghost of him. But this boy didn't look like Sean.

There was a long pause between the two boys beneath the bridge. The new boy continued to speak.

"I like it here. It's quiet, no one bothers me," said the naked child.

"Me too," Devin replied.

"What's your name?"

"Devin... What's yours?"

"Alexander."

"You don't live around here?"

"I don't live anywhere. I'm looking for a home," he said. "Until I find one, I'm staying here."

Devin paused. He had never heard of something like this.

"Where are your parents?"

"Don't know." He shrugged.

"Where are your clothes?"

He shrugged again.

There was a long silence. Devin began to feel bad for the boy.

"You're a little bigger than me, but I can get some clothes for you and bring them to you."

Alexander nodded.

"Just wait here. It will take me a few minutes."

Devin returned with some clothes and an apple. He gave them to Alexander and turned his back as Alexander dressed.

"Sometimes I go skip stones over there," Devin said, pointing to the Trent River.

The boys headed toward the river.

Devin found the smooth stones along the shoreline and sent them over the waves as best he could. Alexander was much better at it. He said he was six, but he seemed not only bigger but older than Devin.

A boat passed, reasonably close to shore. The three young guys in it yelled at the boys. "What are ya doin', ya little losers!? Get out of here! Go home." Devin shrank back, stunned.

Alexander squinted, looked at Devin's worried face, and threw a rock above the waves and high enough that it hit their boat with a loud snap. The guys in the boat started screaming at them. "You little twerps!"

The driver turned the boat towards shore. Alexander began laughing, and Devin started to run. "C'mon! We better go," he said.

The boys scrambled up the bank, and, as they did, Alexander looked over his shoulder.

"Ah, did we scare you? Are you afraid your little boat is gonna sink? Do you not know how to swim? Poor babies!"

Devin pulled on his new friend's shirt, and the boys began to laugh and run along the sidewalk.

"This way," Devin said, "to my house."

Alexander paused on the sidewalk.

"Ok. Don't worry, Alexander. Just stand by me."

The two boys began to settle into a rhythm. They would disappear after breakfast each day to play together alone. Devin wanted to avoid Sean's house and family. It soon became a habit for him to not even look at the home.

Alexander picked up on this and would often take them out the back door so they wouldn't have to see Sean's house, right across the street. They also avoided playing with Sean's siblings. The boys sunk into their world, where no one was invited to join them. Not even Rachel. The boys just had each other.

"Gloomy Sunday"
Billie Holiday

How dare the sun rise? This was Doreen's first thought the morning after the funeral.

It was a bright morning. Birds were singing.

I can't stand the sun and I can't look at the stars.

She groaned.

I know I have to do something with myself. Could I climb into the hole in my chest? Could the emptiness expand until it swallowed me?

She looked at the tip of her finger that was gone now. *Could I be gone? Did I want to enter into that nothingness?* She lay in bed with the question and determining how she could fold her body into this strange, growing gloom.

Doreen's sister, Karen, was still with them and was taking care of the children. Doreen rarely left her room. Karen tried to speak to her about it, but Doreen merely gave her a look to let her know this was not welcome.

Days passed, and Karen finally cornered Doreen at the kitchen counter when her sister was fetching coffee.

"Hey, D."

Doreen didn't answer but just looked at her sister.

"You have a lot to handle. Have you thought about talking to a doctor or a social worker or something?"

Doreen hated this conversation as much as she despised any other attempts people made to speak to her.

"I can help you, but I can't be the mother the kids need. They need you."

"Okay," was all she could muster. It would end the conversation, at least.

I have to step into the world. I can't rely on the black hole to swallow me. Kevin. All I have is anger or ambivalence for you. The best I can give to you is the space from me and my corrosive feelings.

I need to go back to my job. To pay for a space for the children to live in and for food to eat. No more than that. Barely that. The thought of going back to work takes all I've got. I don't want attention. I want to step away from life. To only be in it as required.

She called her boss, Mr. Fleming, and told him she would not be at work the coming Monday. He understood.

"I don't know when for sure. Can you give me a few weeks? A little time?" she asked.

"Of course," he said.

The common ground between her and her husband was dwindling. All that was left was a small patch of burnt earth between them. They didn't try to communicate with one another, and they made no demands of each other. He didn't know about the void in her chest. She hadn't been naked in his presence since the accident.

In the weeks to come, when he would arrive home drunk and want sex, he would find her in a t-shirt, her bra, and the small plastic platter. He never noticed the tiny cover. She would acquiesce when he crawled on to her. She felt that giving in was easier than resisting. Besides, she was never even sure if he could do it. He always wanted it, but some nights it was a feeble attempt that quickly became a snoring man on her chest. The first few times they did have sex, part of her was curious about whether it would allow her to feel something. It didn't. So, for her, his advances became a nuisance, nothing more. And she felt no strong desire for the comfort or relief of intercourse.

The summer days droned on for her. After a few weeks, Doreen returned to work. She began smoking again and was quickly up to a pack a day. She lived mostly on coffee. She sent the kids away as much as possible. The school year was soon to start. On those days, when the children were out and staying overnight somewhere, she would not go home until late at night.

She drove aimlessly on the little highways and backroads until after dark. Sometimes the car radio would keep her company, and sometimes she would turn it off, remove her shirt and bra, and just listen to that rushing sound in her chest, and the wind coming through the windows of the car as she travelled topless in the dark.

"Sodade"
Cesaria Evora

One evening, Doreen had travelled far north — past Highway 7 — and was on a road that wound through the Canadian Shield. She passed a small church she hadn't noticed before.

She slowed the vehicle to a stop on the side of the small country road, waited and then turned. She sat in the parking lot with the car running, staring at the cross on the steeple. The sign for it read "St Lucy's Church."

She turned off the engine and stepped to the front door of the building. Doreen looked back over her shoulder to confirm her car was the only one in the parking lot. She felt foolish to try the door because it would likely be locked. But it wasn't. She stepped over the threshold and listened. No sound came from within. It was a simple country church made of brick with about ten rows of pews on either side of the nave.

Doreen stood at the back, looking up towards the front of the church. She looked around and saw that the lights outside illuminated the stained glass windows. Since she was a child, Doreen had been attracted to stained glass for both the beauty and the story it told. Beneath the image of a woman standing in apparent defiance of a sword-wielding soldier, it read "Sancta Lucia."

The light moved through the stained glass and spread across some of the pews. She was drawn to the light and walked toward it. Standing between the rows of pews, she let the light fall on her. She removed her blouse and bra and even removed the plastic cover. The light disappeared into her body. She took pleasure in watching this. She could feel her knees growing weak and fell to the pew. She slumped on it and then laid on her back while still ensuring the light could fall into her. She stayed there, motionless, and didn't make a sound.

She could feel something happening in her chest, but there were no words for it.

The hardwood pews should not be comfortable, but this is the closest I have felt to ease in the last few months. I love this silence. And this light disappearing in me. Why do I love this so much? Can I feel it?

Doreen woke to the sound of birds and a brighter light coming through the window. She was startled, and she forgot where she was. It was morning.

Where am I? Where am I supposed to be?

She looked at her watch and saw it was just after 6:00 a.m. *I need to get the kids to school...*

"Oh, Sean..."

This longing... a longing that will never be resolved.

And she wept. She put her face on her knees and cried. After half an hour, it subsided, and she began to dress and make her way out of the church, back to her car, and to her house. She arrived just as the children were waking. Kevin was asleep on the living room couch with the TV still going.

As the school year took shape, she assembled a bearable life. Anna had convinced Doreen that she didn't need to go to a babysitter after school. Doreen agreed. So, Anna would make her way home from school and pick up Alicia at the babysitter's house along the way. Her mother would arrive home a little after five.

When Doreen arrived home, she would generally find a meal made by Anna. If she had thought about it, she would have noticed that the dynamic in their home had changed. Anna was taking care of them. Kevin was only there sometimes and Doreen and Anna typically ignored him. Sometimes he would play with the baby.

Each had their own trajectory.

Doreen would have dinner with the children. Often without conversation, and if there was talk, it was minimal and led by the children. When the kids were asleep, she would tell Kevin she was going out and disappear to the church.

She didn't want to disclose her habit to anyone. She went to the same church. It was a ritual: the meandering drive through the countryside, quietly entering the empty church and going to the same pew, unbuttoning her blouse, removing the little shield and her bra, and then allowing the light to fall into the black hole. Each time she would cry and fall down to the wooden bench and lie on it. Sometimes she would lose control when she wept and fall to her knees sobbing. When her tears came to an end, she would often turn to prayer. The prayers from childhood were still there, especially the Lord's Prayer. But it lacked gravity, and her mind searched until she remembered another prayer from her childhood:

Hail, Mary, full of grace,
the Lord is with thee.
Blessed art thou amongst women,
and blessed is the fruit of thy womb, Jesus.
Holy Mary, Mother of God,
pray for us sinners,
now and at the hour of our death.
Amen.

"O ignis Spiritus paracliti"
Hildegaard von Bingen

Doreen's practice continued through the autumn. Whenever she could escape for an evening, she would do so. Sometimes two or three nights a week.

Her secret life was soon to be revealed.

It was a Tuesday in early October when Lydia McCartney entered the church.

Here comes the church mouse, she thought. It made her smile.

Lydia was often alone in the building. She was a petite woman with light brown hair.

Lydia was one of the few volunteers for this tiny house of prayer and had come into it that evening out of curiosity about the car in the parking lot. Driving home, she passed by the building and was surprised to spot it. She was concerned about vandals. Nothing had happened at her church, but she had heard of the problems at other congregations.

In my childhood, we never considered such things. I guess it's because more of us went to the services then. It was busy. We had fewer attendees each year and not many groups associated with the church.

She quietly entered the building, slowly opening the door. There was only silence within. She moved slowly and then caught a glimpse of something she would never forget: a woman, naked from the waist up, and in the middle of her chest, was a hole. The light from the stained-glass window was disappearing into the cavity. It refused to be illuminated. Instead, it seemed to be feeding on those pale beams.

Lydia was shocked and stood there with her amazement.

As she moved past her astonishment, she began to feel as though she had intruded on an intimate act not meant for her. Lydia also felt that speaking to this strange woman would somehow be inappropriate. So, she peered around the doorway into the nave of the church to watch her. And when Doreen began to cry and fell to her knees weeping, Lydia backed out of the church.

That's enough. This poor woman. Give her some space.

Lydia was burdened by this miracle and buoyed by it at the same time. She couldn't bring herself to speak of it. She had read from *Lives of the Saints* as a child and heard of miracles, but this one seemed so strange. Was it even Christian?

The next morning, she was distracted as she prepared her only child, Leslie, for school. Leslie was sixteen and had the growing malaise and restlessness of a teenager in a rural community.

She found her mother both provincial and almost too worldly or compromised.

"Leslie?" she called to her daughter. She paused and waited.

Then again, "Leslie!"

She was growing frustrated, waiting for her daughter, and she was preemptively annoyed by Leslie's attitude.

Finally, Leslie appeared from the bathroom.

"Mom! You've got to relax! I know we have to go!"

Her mother seethed but didn't respond. She turned her back and started towards the door.

"Oh, now I'm the bad guy, right?" Leslie asked.

Lydia was trying her best not to respond.

I don't want to be sucked into this. I have more significant issues to think about...

She carried Doreen's image in the church around with her like a tattoo that no one could see.

"So... like, at worst, I would miss the first part of homeroom. Which is totally pointless anyway," Leslie announced on her way down the stairs.

She couldn't stop herself anymore as they got into the car.

"Yes, Leslie, I know everything here is pointless, and I am pointless, and nothing matters. I should just go jump off a bridge, right?"

Leslie was stunned. Her mother usually gave her a warm but firm reply. She could rarely provoke her mom's anger. She always wanted to see it, but now that she had, her overwhelming feeling was regret. She felt like she'd crossed a line. Leslie fell silent.

"Now, you have nothing to say."

"I'm sorry," Leslie offered.

Lydia could feel the authenticity of the apology and gave her daughter a kiss on the cheek.

"I know, I know you are. I'm sorry I yelled at you," said Lydia.

"Mom, it's just that this place gets to you too, right? Like every day, it's the same. Nothing happens here, and it just feels like nothing matters here."

Lydia's exasperation grew again.

"You matter, but you don't know anything. You can't see the beauty and wonder around you, and that says more about you than this place. The problem isn't that there are no miracles. It's that we won't let ourselves have the eyes to see them. This is a place of miracles too often ignored."

Leslie's jaw slackened. She fell silent.

Lydia surprised herself with these words. She didn't want to say anything else. She wanted her pronouncement to echo. Lydia bathed in that silence all the way to the school where she dropped off her daughter. She was amazed at the words she had spoken. They didn't seem like hers. She felt strengthened by them.

Over the coming days, Lydia grew to love her secret. She found herself driving past the church day and night to see if that car was there again.

Almost two weeks later, when she was driving Leslie home from a piano lesson, she took a longer route to go by the church. She drove onto Hazelton Road, and as she did, she noticed another car turn into the church parking lot. It was just under a kilometer away from them. Lydia slowed as she saw this happen. Her mind began racing as she brought her car to a stop on the side of the road. Her daughter was engrossed in a book and didn't seem to notice her mother had stopped the vehicle.

She waited a moment and then slowly brought the car forward, and as she reached the church parking lot, she turned off the lights. The lot was empty except for that one vehicle. The same one that had been there that night. She was pretty sure. Lydia parked at the edge of the parking lot, as far as possible from the church.

Should I show her? Is it too much? Or is it just the sort of thing that she needs to see, to experience?

Then she turned to her daughter.

"Come with me. I'm going to show you something. You cannot make any noise," she said with gravity.

"Do not speak and be as quiet as possible." Leslie looked up from *One Hundred Years of Solitude* with puzzlement and interest and nodded.

The two women crept across the church parking lot and slowly opened the door of the church.

As they entered, Lydia looked over her shoulder with one finger to her pursed lips. They peaked into the nave. There was a faint, rustling sound. Lydia motioned for Leslie to stop, and she did. She saw the profile of the woman staring up at the stained glass, wearing only a skirt. Lydia motioned for Leslie to join her, pointed, and again gave the signal, once more, to be quiet.

Her chest was not visible to them from their vantage point, but it was clear that she had begun to cry. Her body turned limp and then lifeless. As she began to fall to the pew, Leslie saw the black hole in her chest.

Lydia was mesmerized. She was pulled towards the scene unfolding before her. She shook her head to break the spell as she realized she needed to ensure that her daughter was okay. She quickly looked at her. Leslie's mouth was open, and her eyes were as wide as her own. She hadn't seen her daughter amazed like this in years.

Lydia closed her eyes, and words surfaced from some unseen place and fell from her mouth: "Holy are you, a healing balm to the broken."

The woman in the pew was now sobbing on her knees, and Lydia took Leslie by the wrist and pulled her out of the church. Leslie didn't resist and became a moving object with little care for the force moving her.

They walked quickly but quietly to the car and sat in it for a few moments, speechless. Lydia started the vehicle but did not turn on the lights and drove out of the church parking lot.

Leslie was the first to speak.

"Who was that? What was that?"

There was a long pause before Lydia said anything. Again, the words just emerged and sprung into sound: "A miracle among us."

"O, My Soul"
Big Star

In the days that followed, Lydia and Leslie would pass glances between one another, but neither spoke of the woman in the church. Both women knew what they saw was beyond their shared vocabulary.

The following Saturday night, Leslie had received permission from her parents to go to a house party with her friend, Kim, who had just received her driver's license. They were going to drive to the event to celebrate this accomplishment. It was around seven thirty when Kim arrived at the front door. Leslie was waiting and quickly ran to join her, hollering to her parents as she went out the door.

"All right, I'm going, see you later."

Her father hollered back: "By eleven!"

"Yeah!"

She bounded down the stairs of the front porch to Kim, waiting in the driver's seat of the Dodge Colt.

"Kim! This is amazing! I can't believe you have a car!"

"I know, right?" said her friend, beaming.

Kim turned up the stereo as "Hollywood Nights" boomed through the little vehicle. The girls let out a triumphant squeal. They had to drive about twenty minutes from the town of Moira for the party at Mary MacKenzie's cottage on the Black River near Elzivir.

The church was on the way. Leslie was aware of this when they made plans to go to the party. She was drawn to the church and to the woman.

"Do you want to take a little detour?" she asked hesitantly. "Because if we do, you might see something amazing."

I hope Kim can be cool. She's gotta be cool.

Kim paused for a moment, distracted in her excitement, and said, "Sure." It felt like a night of adventure for her, and this only added to the feeling.

"Okay, as long as it's not too far away, 'cause I have strict rules about where I'm allowed to drive. It's really kind of annoying. Plus, I wanna get to the party!"

"It's on Hazelton Road, which is just a few minutes ahead."

"Okay, well, that's not too bad."

Saturday nights were the nights it was easiest for Doreen to get away. She could get a sitter for the kids, and Kevin was often out with his brother or elsewhere.

She had arrived just as the sun was setting. She thought of this as she parked the car, and how, in the days ahead, there would be a growing darkness outside of her. It was everywhere. Autumn and the coming winter were inevitable.

Leslie was pleased to see the little car in the parking lot. This time she got to be the host, the purveyor of miracles. She told Kim to be quiet and led her into the church.

Kim was shocked. Although Leslie pleaded silently for her to not utter a sound, she could barely keep quiet in the church.

Leslie pulled her out of the church when she was sure her friend wouldn't be able to contain her amazement. As they reached the parking lot, Kim broke her silence.

"My God! Oh, my God! Oh, my God! What did I just see? Did you get me high? Am I high right now? What did you do to me? How did this happen?"

Leslie had started to answer her first question but gave up by the second. Her silence was a rumination on a possible error. Had she made a mistake in bringing Kim here? So, she changed the subject.

"Maybe we should skip the party," she said.

"No way, I'm going," Kim quickly responded.

"Okay... Well, let's not talk about this to anyone there," said Leslie cautiously.

"Why not?" questioned Kim indignantly.

"I don't know... I just... I don't want people to think we're lying or something. They don't get it, or if they do get it, they may be weird about it," Leslie offered with faltering confidence.

Kim didn't answer but started the car. She turned up the stereo. She stopped as she left the parking lot and pulled a cassette tape out of her bag. Debbie Boone. Leslie grimaced at the thought of listening to "You Light Up My Life".

In a few minutes, they were at the party, and she lost Kim.

That night and the days that followed, a murmur spread through Moira and the surrounding area of the woman who swallowed light with her chest. In fact, by Sunday morning, the story was making its way to the congregation of the church itself. At lunch, the minister was being told about it. The myth had grown and was a specter, haunting the church.

So, on the following Tuesday, when she arrived at the church, just after eight that night, Doreen was surprised to find cars in the parking lot. Then she saw the people.

Kim was there, and she pointed at the car and couldn't help exclaiming, "I think that's it! I think that's her!"

People ran towards the car. For Doreen, it quickly became apparent to her what had happened. She had been found out. She was mortified. It didn't take long for her to realize this and that she didn't want it.

She quickly stomped on the gas pedal in her Datsun, sending dust and gravel in the air of the lot, and swerved around yelling people to make it to the exit.

I did not want an audience. I didn't ask for company. I tried to hide it away. This is for me. This is for Sean.

She sped through the country roads until she was sure no one was following her. She realized she was on the edge of some old Crown lands just off Juniper Road. Her father liked to tell her stories of his adventures in the forests, and she remembered that one that started with the "The Crown lands just off Juniper Road..."

There are so many forests here that they seem forgettable. They aren't even given names.

She pulled down what looked like a forgotten road to make sure she was out of sight. She got out of the car and began to wander into the woods. The sun was setting when she stopped, and she leaned against a towering ash tree.

Doreen looked up and marveled at the change of season — the celebration of the leaves.

Every year it takes my breath away.

Immediately after thinking that, she realized it was the first time she felt really anything other than a desperate sadness that pulled her and held her down. She fell to her knees crying and offered a prayer in two words: "Thank you."

"The Lark Ascending"
Ralph Vaughan Williams

At work the next day, Doreen began devising a new plan.

I'm not here to be anybody's freak or miracle. I don't want anything from anyone... I'm just trying to survive. That's it.

She then burst into tears at her desk.

Oh my god. Not here. I don't want them to see me like this.

She made it to the bathroom, found a stall, and wept.

After a few minutes, her mind worked towards a solution: *the time in that quiet forest felt so similar to that moment in the church...*

A few days later, she went back there. She started going to the woods regularly. Always a different forest. And when she removed her clothing, the experience would return, especially on nights when the moon shined brightly on her.

Word had reached her in Scott's Mills about the miraculous woman. Fortunately, the fifty kilometers between the village and that church was enough of a distance that no one connected it to her. So, as the weather grew colder and the sun set earlier, she found herself going to the forests early in the evening, before work, or on her lunch.

As winter came, and the nights began early, she started to search for churches again. But she would never visit the same church twice. She couldn't risk others spotting her.

She also began to reflect on what she was doing.

I know I need this, but I don't actually know what this is. Is this the end of me or the start of something new? Have I gone mad?

She decided not to tell anyone. Anyone she could trust, she wanted to keep at a distance, for now.

At times she would cry as she undressed, and there were times when she would feel great comfort in the event and all she witnessed. And for that, she would feel tremendous guilt.

What right do I have to feel happy? She shook her head.

As the anniversary of Sean's death approached, Doreen's sister reminded her of the need to write a memorial and for the family to visit the grave. Doreen found it only made her anxious.

What can I offer? What can I say?

She felt like something broken and spent—like dead grass revealed after the winter. She didn't know that she was changing once again.

That June morning, she woke early, showered and made the trek to the convenience store to purchase the day's newspaper.

She forced herself to eat a small breakfast of burnt toast and black coffee.

I can't avoid it. It's best if I read this while the others are still sleeping.

She slowly ate and read Sean's memorial in the Trentonian.

It feels like a story about someone else's child – this poor family.

The children stirred upstairs. She sighed and let the newspaper fall from her hands, stood, and began the process of preparing them for the day.

Obligation. Today is for the living. Not for the dead. I feel I owe all of you very little. I can't even really think about what I am to them. What I should be.

Most of the day, she said little. She offered no words of explanation or comfort to the two girls. Kevin had been gone for at least two days, and she was happy he wasn't home and that she didn't have to bring him to the memorial service with her.

Grief is a lonely road.

Both the graveyard and Sean's plot seemed foreign to her. The baby cooed and pursued the flowers among the graves. Anna stared quietly at the stone, and tears ran from her eyes, past the crow's feet, over her cheekbones and from her jaw to the ground.

After a few minutes, Doreen bent down on her knees and kissed the small gravestone with two angels that marked Sean's resting place.

I've been grieving so privately that this public act feels awkward, like weak coffee on a morning with no sleep.

She left the kids with her sister and escaped to another forest setting.

I just need to be alone.

She found quiet Crown lands just south of Highway Seven. Kneeling beneath the trees, the light was softened by the leaves. A light wind moved through. She could feel herself swoon. She removed her clothing and the covering. Her eyes closed, her body loosened, she let herself fall to the ground. Lying on her back, she stripped herself of all her clothes. Now nude, she was suddenly startled by a flash.

What is that light? Where is it coming from? Me?
Her torso beamed, and even the rest of her was shining like the sun—from the light within and without. She looked down and saw that the world was an overwhelming dazzle of brightness and movement. Everything was alight, and the illumination itself was the matter that formed the objects in her sight: the sturdy grey ash was ablaze and dancing, the shy larks swam in the air, and their bodies swam with light, her body hummed and formed a starry voice ascending then circling round and round in the form of her...

Overcome, she closed her eyes. And then she covered her chest. Her world returned to what she knew. But she was changed.

"My god. Oh, my god," she whispered to herself.

Quiet fell.

She quickly looked down at her torso and noticed the unilluminated space was gone. She was in shock.

She touched her chest and confirmed the black hole had disappeared from her body.

She wept and spoke aloud.

"I can't stop anything from happening," she announced between sobs.

"I'm so sorry, Sean...I'm so sorry I let this happen... I'm sorry I didn't know what to do today. I left everyone. I failed everyone..."

She then fell into a prayer that was one word repeated. "Love, love, love, love, love, love, love..." It ended with one sentence: "My darling boy, I love you so much." She raised her head and offered a kiss to the air or some unseen presence. She stood, looked around the scene, and listened.

The June night is warm, Doreen thought to herself. *The start of summer. It feels like the summers of my youth. Something is over. Something new is beginning. I love beginnings.*

Doreen dressed and slowly made her way home, travelling slowly but with direction. As she drove, she touched her chest. She realized she had put the cover on her chest when she dressed without thinking.

It's a habit, I suppose, to put that plastic on myself. To hide.

She undid a few buttons, removed the covering and touched her chest. She flung the plate out the window.

Her sister left, and Doreen floated through the house, looking at the pictures on the walls and shelves, and then she watched her daughters sleep together in Anna's bed. She joined them. Doreen tilted her head. There was a light that surrounded her two daughters' faces, and she only felt love for them. She kissed them gently on their foreheads.

She woke before them and made breakfast for the girls. She assumed Kevin was asleep on the couch and was surprised to find he wasn't there. Her body felt calm — the first time in over a year.

Anna was shocked and a little annoyed with her mother's presence in the kitchen.

Doreen coaxed them to join her for breakfast. She barely touched her toast and coffee. She mostly watched the baby and Anna.

"Anna, you look different," she said and touched the girl's cheek.

Both her daughters were bewildered by their mother but welcomed her return in the days that followed.

Doreen sat at the table and listened to her family speak. She could still hear the faint sound of rushing wind. She touched her hand to her chest. It was solid. But she knew somehow that sound and that feeling would always remain with her.

Years later, Doreen would read a news report about a scientific paper that described a theoretical phenomenon called a White Hole. It argued that our whole universe is created from the death of a star. A supernova collapsed, shrunk, and formed a black hole, and then burst into a stream of light carrying the matter that formed all we know and can see.

Her thoughts this morning after the funeral were interrupted by a phone call. Anna answered and handed it to her mom with a grave expression and three words: "They found dad."

"A Pair of Brown Eyes"
The Pogues

Kevin made a pact with himself after the funeral. It was actually the day after his appearance at Steve's party. The words of the pledge were like hungry words on the wind, demanding of him: "Keep drinking until you find him and bring him home."

Alcohol was the ingredient that brought Sean to him the night of the funeral, so he was committed to the substance and its path to his son. So, he began to drink heavily in the months following Sean's death. He couldn't share this plan with anyone, but that was his mission.

This time, I will take him back home with me. Doreen and her family are looking after the other two. I'll get Sean. I'll bring him home. I'm his father. I didn't keep Sean safe from harm. I failed. This is my family. Sean is my boy. Now Sean is dead, and I'm to blame. It's as simple as that. But he's coming back to me. Next time he does, I'll take him home. I'll drink every goddamn bottle of booze I find if I need to... and then I can protect him. What else is there to do?

For months now, he was drinking alone and waiting for Sean. He had moments when he would see his boy and would reach out to him only to find himself unable to grasp him. Kevin would wake each time without his son and relive the loss and shame all over again.

As the anniversary of Sean's death approached, Kevin grew more desperate. It was a deadline for him. It was also a reminder that he had not accomplished this singular task.

The rest of his life was in disarray. He had lost his job after showing up hungover and drunk for work and for passing out on a job site more than once. Then there were days that he missed his shift. The foreman was understanding for the first few months, but after six months of absences, drunken days, and outbursts, he let Kevin go.

Kevin didn't mind. He turned all his focus to his mission.

I'll have more of a chance to find Sean now. I'll double my efforts. I can do it at least three days a week. I'll take a day off between sessions to recuperate.

This continued for a few months, but he still hadn't brought Sean home. The anniversary of Sean's death loomed on the quickly approaching horizon. For the last three weeks, he had been drinking even more regularly. Days faded into each other, as did the nights. He rarely ate. He was losing his hair. He felt weak. But he persisted. He gave up on beer, except in the mornings, and drank whiskey.

The night before the memorial service, he stayed at his son's grave again.

That's where it all began. And it's been a year. Maybe he's ready. He taught us a lesson. I hear ya, Sean.

But Sean never arrived. As the sun came up, Kevin woke cold with dew on him. Alone. "Goddamn it," he hollered to no one. He punched the air. He then looked around, to the gravestones. He felt bad for yelling.

"I'm sorry to disturb you."

He came up with a new plan.

This is it. This is the last day to find my boy and bring him home. If I don't get it done, I'm done.

He drove home to get a few hours of sleep before he would start his final charge. He woke just after 11:00 a.m., pulled on jeans and a t-shirt, grabbed his wallet and keys, the last Molson Export in the fridge, and headed out the door.

His truck wouldn't start.

It's the goddamn alternator. Of all the days. Perry from up the street — he always leaves the keys in the truck. Perry wouldn't mind. He would understand, at least. And if he didn't, well, screw him.

No one was at his neighbour's house, so he jumped into the driver's seat and found the keys under the seat where Perry always kept them. He quickly started the vehicle, backed out of the driveway and was gone.

Maybe I need to look for you somewhere new. Tricky little bastard.

He drove to the liquor store in Trenton, grabbed a bottle of Crown Royal, and carried on towards Belleville along Highway 2.

He stopped for a while and sat by the Marysville bridge to Prince Edward County. He loved this long, high bridge that went over the lake. The views were majestic. He then decided to climb the bridge. With a whiskey bottle in hand, he walked along the pedestrian portion until he reached the highest point. The wind was warm, and it was quiet. He scanned the world around him. He could be anywhere. Kevin closed his eyes and then looked down. Part of him wanted to continue to lean forward. Instead, he took a long drink from the bottle.

"Not yet..."

He turned back and climbed down the bridge. When he reached Napanee, he took the road heading south of the town to catch Loyalist Parkway, so he could drive along the lake. He reached the road and continued to Kingston. The bottle was getting empty as he reached the city, so he drove into the downtown core to the liquor store.

"I'm sorry, sir, but we aren't allowed to serve you if you've already been drinking."

"I only drink to breathe."

"Sir?"

"Ya gotta help me out."

"I don't know how I can do that."

"I need to see my boy. I'm going to see my boy."

"I'm sorry."

"Don't be sorry. I'm takin' it."

Kevin snatched the bottle and threw some bills down on the counter.

"Don't worry, I'm almost done," he said to no one in particular. As he gained his footing, he was struck by the thought of the years that the brown eyes of Sean stood waiting for him.

He tried to sprint out the door but ran into the frame, knocked himself backward. His knees started to give out. Kevin steadied himself and carried on.

So much darkness. It comes and goes. I guess that left turn coming out was wide.

Honking.

Screw you. The damn bottle won't open. It doesn't even burn anymore. Oh shit, that's my fault. His lane. But screw him. Screw these cars. The bottles on the floor sound like a song. What's that song? That's no song. That's Sean. Go, dad, go, dad. That's right, Sean. Let's take her up to the 401 so we can really go, Sean. Let's show them. We ain't afraid of any cars, now, are we, son?"

"Swordfishtrombones"
Tom Waits

For Amy McMurtry, the sight was one of pure madness.

She was driving home from her shift as a nurse at Kingston General Hospital. Tired, she had to make conscious efforts to stay awake.

Crackin' the window isn't goin' to do it.

She grabbed the handle and turned it clockwise until the window was fully down.

It still smells like morning. I love June.

She breathed in deeply and closed her eyes for a moment. She opened them to see a truck driving straight at her. The vehicle was coming down the off-ramp at the Joyceville exit of the four-lane, 401 Highway.

She shook her head.

Am I seeing things? No. They're driving the wrong way. Whoever it is, is going to collide with the traffic.

The road was meant to be a way off the highway, not an entrance. She waved her arm out the window, flashed her headlights and even accidentally turned on her windshield wipers.

I ain't moving for anyone. Screw 'em. Right, Sean? Goddamn right! Watch out! I got a party in my head!

As she swerved to avoid the oncoming motorist, she felt a strong need to know who was behind the wheel.

Who in the hell would do this?
As the truck swung past her, all she could see was the crazed face of a man with one hand on the wheel and the other

raised to her with a middle finger standing alone. He was screaming. He continued down the highway another three kilometers, screaming out the window and sipping from his bottle.

It's time we go off-roading, my boy.

He took his foot off the gas, pumped the brake and turned the wheel hard to the left. Dust flew as he hit the gravel. The truck spun around and then shot over the ditch, through a rickety wire fence, and into a field.

"Whooo! Okay. All right."

The bottle of whiskey shot from Kevin's lap. He tried to grab it, let go of the wheel, and took his foot off the gas, and the truck continued through the field with no one guiding it, slowing, and hitting a Jack Pine in a patch of small trees and shrubs that brought it all to a halt. Kevin was knocked to the floor and didn't move.

"Gymnopédies no. 3"
Erik Satie

About four hours later, Kevin woke to find himself somewhere between a dream and this place. He could sense his son's presence but couldn't see him anywhere. Before he even opened his eyes, he was muttering.

"Sean, Sean... are you there, my boy? I know you're here... Sean?"

He heard no reply. The silence formed a knife that cut into him, past his chest bone, and into his heart.

"I'm done."

If he weren't already lying down, he would have fallen down. Instead, he began to vomit. He just pushed open the door of the pickup truck and heaved from his position on the floor. He clambered up to the bench seat. Looking around the truck, he felt desolate. He saw the creek bed just a few feet away. Dry, cracked, spent and rendered useless. Still laying across the seats, he reached for the bottle of Crown Royal. He felt a flash go off inside his head and then another.

Have I been electrocuted?

He had spasms in his body and could see a jarring light. Then it just stopped.

It's night? No one's here. Where am I? Sean...? I've never felt more disappointed in myself... If I'm dying, he must be here. I'll find you, Sean. It feels like swimming. My boy, my boy? I can't speak. If I could cry, I would now. I give up. Oh, Sean, where are you?

He wept.

Goodbye.

He let himself drift and drift in a pool of such deep, dark despondency that he was shocked when light appeared on the horizon.

What's that? It's too bright. My god, that hurts. Oh, my god. It's all too much – all of this light. I don't want it. Who is that? Is that Sean? No. Who is that? Those voices are like music. Here I am! Right here. I'm not alone. I don't wanna be alone no more...

When he woke, he saw Alicia, Anna, and Doreen. He wept to find them with him. And he wept for Sean's absence. He stared at the three of them for a long time. Neither his wife nor his daughters spoke. Alicia crawled around his legs. He loved it. He felt something. Even if it was just on one side of his body. Then he cried. The tears only fell from one eye. From the side of his body that was not impacted by the stroke

"Soooooo-eeeeee...Soooooooooo-eeeeeee" he muttered.

Only half of his mouth worked, but Doreen and Anna knew from his crying eye, and the partially formed words, what he was trying to say. They knew what he meant. He would have a weeping eye for weeks. In the days that followed, he would be treated by doctors, nurses, therapists, and councilors, and visited by the police. He wouldn't be charged for the theft of the truck. Perry refused to press charges. Anna helped his case. She explained the story. She spoke about the death of her brother and her father's sadness in a matter-of-fact tone.

As Kevin gained consciousness, Anna spoke to her father.

"Dad, we have exercises at 7:00, breakfast at 7:45, and then mom needs to drop me at school at 8:15. During the day, the nurse will come at 10:00 a.m. I will be home just after 3:00. I have to pick up the baby. I can make dinner and work on your speaking then. It will take some time to come back from a stroke, but you can do it."

Kevin tried to nod his head in submissive agreement while crying a single lane of tears down his face. Her mother was quiet. She just stroked her daughter's hair; she lay a hand upon Kevin's chest. As she felt the faint beating, her own heart had a slight quickening.

PART II

"The Stolen Child"
The Waterboys

With those final words, the storyteller pushed back from the table.

"You mean, that's it?"

"Well, that's never *it*. There's always more. What do you want to know?"

"For starters, what happened to you. Or... the two boys?"

"It's getting late. They're gonna wanna close up here soon. Maybe we should do this another time."

"Can we go somewhere else?"

"Okay. Sure. I want to show you something anyway. It might help you."

"Okay. Should we grab a drink for the road?"

He laughed. "I better drive. Let's just take a breather from the story."

"Where are we going?"

"You'll see."

We took the Thousand Islands Parkway to Stoneport and then Highway 2 as we exited the town. As we drove into Kingston around 1:00 a.m., he revealed our destination.

"We're going to take the Loyalist Parkway. You know, the road that follows the lake on the other side of Kingston. We're going to Cashell Island. I've got a place out there."

"I remember going out there once as a kid. It's pretty."

There was a ferry to the island. We caught the 1:30 a.m. boat.

It was a bright evening. There was a full moon on the rise. Lake Ontario was quiet. The only sound was our boat disturbing the waters in the night. No other soul had joined us in the crossing.

We drove out of the village of Estelle, where the ferry arrived, following the small road west. The island was quiet too—a few scattered houses, farms, fields, and forests. After about five kilometers, the small paved road turned into a dirt road. We continued along this road for another five minutes until we reached the end of the gravel and one last house. It was an old limestone house sitting on a large tract of land, looking out at the water and the mainland. It was night, but I could tell it was a special place. I had always loved these old limestone homes. I could hear livestock moving in the fields. The stars gleamed brightly in this rural place.

"My god, this is beautiful."

"I hoped you'd feel that way. Let's walk out to the bluffs."

We hiked parallel to the shore, for about a kilometer, to the western tip of the island. There was magic at play. Here, the forests quit and rolling green lands tapered down to slabs of limestone that jutted into the lake. At some points, cliffs formed, overlooking the waters. The moonlight illuminated it all.

This island, I thought, *just twenty kilometers of earth folded into a lake, but seems so strange and rare. Otherworldly.* I was immediately smitten with this place.

Voices surfaced: *Come away, human child.*

From where? Within or without? It was like a chorus of sounds. I stopped and looked around. No one.
"You can hear that, can't you?"

I nodded.

To the waters and the wild.

"You may have noticed that we went through the hamlet of Dingle just before we arrived here. It's only a little way down the road from us. It was named by the Irish settlers of the island. This part of it had a lot of Irish immigrants. Some of them were your family. And people say that when they came here, the little people as they called them, stowed away on ships and made it to Canada, as well. The fairies. In these quiet forests and dells, they found a new home."

Away with us, he's going, the solemn eyed.

"They're mischievous things. They lead you astray. Sometimes your disheveled head needs to be led away, though, doesn't it?"

I nodded. My world was spinning. Where was I? Who was I? What was this?

He had moved ahead, picked a spot on a cliff, sat down, and patted the grass beside him. I stood enchanted and confused. The voices faded. I didn't know what else to do, and my legs were getting weak, so I joined him. As I sat, he began again.

"School Days"
Kate and Anne McGarrigle featuring
Loudon III, Rufus and Martha Wainwright

He sat cross-legged, perched on the cliff. He closed his eyes and breathed deeply, exhaled, then raised his right arm and pointed to the west.

"It was just over there. About sixty kilometers from here."

I nodded. He began.

-

In the days and months following the accident, Devin and Alexander carried their secret together. It bonded them, but they were alone with it. When Devin's parents would speak to him about it, he would grow silent and sullen. The boys rarely even talked to each other about it. Devin's dad moved up the ladder at the Royal Canadian Mounted Police and had a new job in Ottawa. Just two months after the accident, they moved. It was a suburb of the city that they would call home — Nepean. It was filled with working-class families, some new Canadians. They lived across the road from the Bayshore Shopping Centre. They had never seen anything like it — its massive size and all the treasures it contained. Alexander had less interest in being inside the mall than he did in the four-storey parking lot. Not long after they moved into their townhouse, Alexander convinced Devin to ride their new BMX bikes over to the shopping complex on a Sunday morning. Alexander was adamant that he and Devin needed them after the accident. Devin was resistant. But his parents relented and made the purchase. The stores were closed on Sundays, which meant the boys could ride through the building's five floors with few cars to bother them.

"We can ride to the top of the parking garage and then speed all the way down! It'll be awesome," Alexander exclaimed.

Alexander pedaled fast to the top floor. Devin followed more slowly behind him. Alexander was waiting for him, and as Devin arrived, Alexander took off down the ramp.

"See ya!" he said and was quickly riding into the dark recesses. Devin said nothing but turned and followed. Alexander loved it. Going down the ramps, he let himself be pulled faster and faster through the spiral to the bottom. Each corner he turned was blind. He didn't know what would be there — a car, a person? The bike was shaking, the corners were hard to make the closer he got to the end, but Alexander refused to be afraid. He growled and howled.

"YOOOOWWWW!" echoed through the empty building.

He would breathe deeply, grit his teeth and make the turns at top speed. The rear tire of his bike would skid across the cement at each corner. He knew he was fighting something, but he didn't have a name for what it was. It was a feeling within and a presence that was lurking near him. An entity he detested, and if he could turn his head quickly enough, he just might see, but it always disappeared. He could feel it near him as he was pulled down and down into dark rooms made of cement. If that thing or fear was to come to him, he had decided to meet it with a resounding "NO! You cannot scare me again. You cannot hold me, contain me, chase me, or haunt me. I am greater than you. You will never scare me again. Never."

His young life would continue like this: racing, challenging, and growing in strength. Within a year, they would move to the country. He would stir up the herds of cattle in the fields until that bored him, and he moved on to playing chicken with cars, finding bullies and those in power he deemed foolish, and squaring off with them. It came to an end at the age of seventeen, when he was finally outnumbered and left for dead in a ditch.

Alexander reached the bottom, hit the brakes and screeched to a halt with his back wheel sliding sideways and the bike teetering. But he managed to gain control and come to a stop. He was panting with his legs spread wide over his BMX when Devin arrived. Devin had tried to follow Alexander's lead but found himself riding the brake. Touching it throughout the ride and not really enjoying it.

"Awesome, right?" said Alexander.

Devin just smiled and nodded his head. He was tired. He found he was often exhausted. And he was too young to know that children didn't typically have dreams like the ones he had. Visions that left him not only bothered in the day but worn out. They had begun only a few days after the accident. The dreams were flashes of the accident, of course. Often it was just the front tire of the bike rolling on its own along the road. He would hear noises. These flashes would often happen as he slipped into sleep, and he would wake panting in his room. The adrenaline coursing through his body would keep him awake at night. He wouldn't reach out to his parents or sister for comfort because that would mean that he would have to explain his dreams and why they were troubling him. A wave of shame and fear washed over him at the thought of telling anyone. Devin wanted reprieve, release from this pain, and he wanted shelter.

A year after moving to Ottawa, Devin's father received another promotion. It meant they needed to move again. This time it was to the countryside just north of the St. Lawrence River, outside Stoneport.

It was a summer day in late June when they moved to their new home in the country. After the chaos and excitement of the day wore off, Devin left his family, the moving truck, and all the boxes. It was dusk. He wandered from their new house out to the road, across it, and to the forest that faced their new home. He had never lived in the countryside before, but it awakened a great hunger that it also simultaneously sated.

Devin moved towards the wilds, hesitantly. Strange smells were wafting in the air. The summer breeze blew warm. His hands brushed the top of long grass, Queen Anne's Lace, and buttercups on the edge of the woods. The sun was illuminating the forest. Brightening all it could reach. Songbirds were singing strange ditties. He caught sight of chipmunks wrestling. He ventured further into the woods, to the crest a hill filled with maple trees and far from the sight of anyone. When he reached the peak, he was astonished to look below and find a forest floor covered in pristine white trilliums. The flowers went on and on. It was beautiful and still. He trembled and was moved to tears.

I want to stay here with these pale little flowers.

He sensed that life was a current moving him and this moment was a reprieve in a pool at the edge of that river. Upstream was death, sorrow, and shame. Downstream? Who knew? It was then that he realized it was a year since Sean had died. He had just finished grade one, so the anniversary would be around now. He laid down on the edge of the field of trilliums and wept.

He couldn't help feeling like he had still done something wrong. Something for which he couldn't forgive himself or explain to others in hopes of comfort and understanding. What had happened was too terrible to be forgotten. He couldn't allow himself to forgive or forget. It was like a hunger that could not be sated. *What could I do?*, he thought. Life was waiting for him, and he wanted to stay away from it. He wanted to stay here. He then realized that no one could take this away from him — this retreat. He'd never had this before. It buoyed him and allowed him to return home, knowing he could slip away and be back here in the morning.

Life in the country was a balm to the boy. Sometimes Devin would wait until dusk and wander alone outside. He was amazed by the stars. In them, he would find hope, and in the quiet, he would imagine all of the people in his home preparing for bed. Their peace brought him joy.

He would watch the animals as shadows moving quietly in the night. It was a time of reflection and questions for him: *Were these creatures as amazed as I am by the change of day to night and the stars? Where would I go from here? Why was I born here and not there? Am I me and not you? Not one bit of me is you?*

Here Devin found the spiritual world. He could sense the deeper world surfacing through the cracks formed from the realityquake a year before. His world would brighten, and he felt the flow in it. It would swell in him. He could barely contain his wonder, joy… and love. Love for everything around him. He was without language for it yet. The sumacs glowed red with love, the wind carried songs of it, the trees stood so mighty with this feeling. He found refuge in books and music. He read voraciously, alone in the countryside, visiting the library every week or two to gather more books. Both of his parents were music lovers, and he would sit alone in the rec room listening to their albums. He started collecting his own, as well.

This made him strange, out of step with most of his classmates. He was aware of it and did little to alter himself to be more palatable. As he grew into a teenager, he dressed in a way that expressed his separateness, with thrift store bowling shirts, ripped jeans, and long hair. When asked to speak, he enjoyed the mental exercise of answering with a song lyric, poems, or an excerpt from a book.

A typical exchange would go like this:

English Teacher, discussing Hamlet's madness: "Devin, we haven't heard from you. Can you share your thoughts?"

Devin: "Although the masters make the rules for the wise men and the fools, I've got nothin', ma, to live up to..."

A silence would descend over the classroom.

Devin smirked. He could sense the confusion and distance that was growing between him and those in the room. And he felt satisfied.

"Lungs"
Townes Van Zandt

"I don't like parties," Alexander offered with a sigh.

"I know, I know. I never see you at any," replied Helena.

Alexander had a hard time refusing Helena. Most of the guys in their grade twelve class liked her. It wasn't just her body, the stars dancing in her eyes, or her kindness. It was her vulnerability. She seemed to injure easily. Alexander wanted to be a moat around her.

Helena had a habit of over-drinking. She pulled Alexander into a room at a house party once and began to drunkenly confess her feelings for him.

"You're so confusing..."

"Am I?" Alexander asked, amused.

"Yeah..." she tilted her head up to him for a kiss and closed her eyes.

Alexander had been drinking and smoking pot but was nowhere near as drunk as Helena. He kissed her forehead and took her hand. He knew this was Joanne's bedroom. The host of the party.

"Come on, Helena."

"Okay. You know best, don't you?"

He led her to the bed. She looked down at it and quickly climbed beneath the top sheet. She pulled Alexander down to her. He sat on the edge of the bed, leaned towards her, and kissed her lightly on her forehead.

"What do I do with you?" she whispered to Alexander.

Alexander smiled but said nothing and pulled a blanket from the bottom of the bed up and around her. She moaned a little and began to fall asleep.

She really is beautiful. She'll likely forget all of this tomorrow.

She was asleep when he left to find Joanne to let her know that Helena was in there. Joanne wanted to move her to another room and asked Alexander for help with it. As he walked Joanne back to where Helena was sleeping, he opened the door to find Rick Mabee on top of the sleeping Helena, with his face on her neck, and his hands moving beneath the blankets.

For Alexander, the world around him faded. There was no music, laughter, or voices. He sprung at Rick. Alexander threw him against the closet door. It nearly broke. Rick lay prone on the floor. Silent. He was trying to get up when Alexander kicked him in the stomach. He paused and then pulled his arm back to punch Rick once more when his elbow hit something. He turned to see Helena reeling backward. He quickly spun around to help her.

Sound returned.

She was yelling.

"What are you doing?" she hollered, with a hand over her right eye. Joanne was also bellowing at him.

He ran through the party and outside. Joanne's house was in the country, and Alex got a ride there with friends but thought he would walk the five kilometers or so to get home. He looked back. No one was following him. Alexander continued but stopped twice while he considered returning to check on Helena but then kept walking. He had covered about two kilometers when Rick and his friends came upon him in a minivan. Alexander stopped in his tracks.

I don't feel anything. No, I do. Regret. Disgust.

The four young men circled him, taunting him. Alexander remained silent. He offered no response or made an effort to prepare for his own defense. Someone kicked him hard in the back of his right leg behind his knee. Alexander fell forward. As he fell, fists and more feet rained down on him.

Be quiet. Give them nothing.

His silence infuriated the young men. The beating continued until Alexander was unconscious.

He heard a voice: "Throw him in the ditch."

Alexander wasn't sure what happened next, but the guys and the van were gone when he woke up. He didn't want to leave the ditch. He dropped his face into the water. He tried to drown in it. He drank in the liquid. He kept drinking until he expelled it. He coughed and then vomited. "Fine," he said and pulled himself up from the water. He didn't want anyone near him, so he walked through the fields, cold and wet, until he was on the outskirts of the village.

It's hard to believe this land will be beautiful again. Everything is grey and brown now. A rough rock-strewn meaninglessness. Trees that look like death.

A kilometer or so behind their elementary school, in a field at the edge of the village, was a deserted farmhouse. He made his way there. It was an old brick building built in the nineteen twenties that had long-since been abandoned. Only the outer brick structure remained as a shell. The glass from the windows was gone, along with the entire second floor. However, most of the floorboards on the main floor, and a set of stairs to a root cellar were intact. The old fireplace still stood.

Alexander had recently started smoking and had a lighter in his pocket, along with his wet cigarettes. He gathered up some old leaves, and garbage sticks from outside, and started a fire. It smoked a little until he found a branch and poked around in the chimney and an old bird's nest fell from within it. He lay on the ground, beside the fire, waiting for sleep.

He spoke to the flames: "I tried."

"Tom Joad, Part 2"
Woody Guthrie

Ralph Sweeney was repairing fences when he smelled something strange.

It was just after dawn, and he had come out to inspect the barriers before he moved some of his cattle into the field. The winter's snow could hide breaks in the metal wires, and now that it was gone, and before he brought his cows into the area, he wanted to be sure he wouldn't lose them to a gap in the enclosure.

Alexander had woken with the light of dawn and the noisy starlings to find himself cold. So, he started another fire with scraps of wood near the house. Ralph was only a few hundred metres from the building and followed the smell. The Sweeney family had owned the land and buildings for three generations. About thirty years before, there had been a house fire that had done a great deal of damage to the building. It had remained deserted since that time. Ralph ventured into the house and found Alexander staring into the fire.

"Hello?"

"Yeah."

"You okay?"

"Yeah..."

"Then what are ya doing here?"

"Listening to the starlings. I prefer birds to the blather of people."

"Can't say I blame you... You want a ride home?"

"I'd like to stay here."

"Well, there ain't much *here,* here."

"Enough for me."

"Well, your folks will be missing ya."

"Will they?"

"I'd imagine so... besides, you look pretty roughed up."

Alexander had a splitting headache from his broken nose, his ribs hurt with each breath, and he was covered in blood. He hadn't thought about how this would look to another person.

Silence sat between the two people.

My god, he looks terrible. He's taken a beating. I get it. There's peace in the fields and the forests. I know him. He isn't a bad kid.

"I'll make you a deal."

"What's that?"

"You can come out here as much as you like as long as you do no damage, and I don't hear about it from your folks."

Alexander knew he couldn't ask for more. He nodded.

"And you let me get you home so they can fix you up."

Ralph gave Alexander a ride home in his truck. They only spoke about the directions to the house. When Alexander reached their house, he turned to Ralph.

"You sure it's okay if I go out there?"
"Yup."

"Because I will."

"Good."

Devin had heard about what happened at the party. He wasn't there, but there had been some phone calls from his friends.

"I can't live inside anymore," is all he offered Devin as he entered the house.

Alexander became a squatter on the deserted farm. He refused to have his broken nose straightened beyond the work done by the local doctor he was forced to visit. Its sudden left turn was softened a little but still visible. He would escape to the wilds outside the village and stay in the house whenever he could. As high school came to a close, he started to work for Ralph on the farm. When chores were scarce, he joined and then led a team that built and maintained trails in the nearby provincial park. Ralph let him fix up the old house, and by the first winter after finishing school, Alexander moved in. He had some basic plumbing, a fireplace, panes of glass in the windows and a few sticks of furniture. When he wasn't working, he read widely, tended his garden, played music, hunted, and fished.

Devin would visit him. Bringing beer, CDs, and, on one occasion, a nicer guitar. They wouldn't talk about much but let the songs they sang speak for them. Before Devin left for university, he went to Kingston and purchased books on agriculture, forestry, and soils, along with hunting and fishing magazines. He also purchased the Loeb Classical Library—a collection of Greek and Roman literature. It was his parting gift to Alexander.

He visited him at the old house one last time. After a half dozen Molson Exports and a dozen songs of increasing sadness were played on his guitar, Devin mustered the strength to ask him what he really wanted to ask Alexander.

"Why are you... I mean, are you happy staying out here?"

Alexander glanced out the window, then down at the instrument in his hands, started strumming his guitar, and without looking up, gave his answer.

"I don't wanna hurt no one."

Devin didn't know what to say. There was nothing he could say. There wasn't a thing he could do. He listened to Alexander play a song by Woody Guthrie. A song he always loved.

"Everybody might just be one big soul..."

Alexander seems older. And he seems to be in the grasp of this place, and it can age you, Devin thought.

"Between The Bars"
Elliott Smith

When Devin reached university, he felt at home. He chose York University for its writing program and to be in Toronto. He found his people. He thrived. He was on the Dean's list, he was a writer at the student paper where he would become the editor and develop a large circle of friends.

Near the end of university, Devin dated his close friend, Mia. A form of love grew between them. She was kind, gentle and urbane. She had been raised in Toronto, and her family quickly adopted Devin. A sense of belonging grew in his life. It was new and strange to Devin. After university, they moved in together.

Devin got a job in the city as a writer and editor for a local magazine, and Mia was a teacher. Life was good, but there were many evenings before he went to bed where he could feel a hollowness within him, and the distance between his new life and himself would become starkly apparent. Disturbing images were stuck in his head of all he had known. It was though the person he was before was out there, waiting for him. And that story was waiting for him.

To do what?

Still, he continued on. He and Mia would marry and have a daughter, Lily. Being a father brought him joy, and that also surprised him. He found himself to be a doting dad and quickly placed Lily at the centre of his life.

Devin rarely visited his home and only spoke to Alexander on rare occasions. Alexander had been farming with the Sweeney's and living the same life he had when Devin left him years ago. The men would see each other about once or twice a year when Devin visited the area. As the years went by, his visits were less frequent, and Alexander never came to the city.

As Devin's thirty-second birthday approached, Mia noticed an increasing restlessness in her husband. She could tell he loved being a father; she loved to watch him with Lily. He was so tender and so clearly enamored with his daughter. But she sensed a restlessness in him. He was frustrated with where they lived. He was unsatisfied with his career. He had grown from a writer and editor to a strategist for campaigns, NGOs and some businesses. His growing successes seemed to bring him little happiness or pride. She knew the restlessness signaled deeper problems. It was as though there was a large splinter trapped beneath his skin. He was trying to live with it, but it only caused a growing discomfort that he was having difficulty managing.

His marriage confounded him. He respected Mia, but he kept her at bay. There was a distance between them he couldn't travel. She knew nothing about the accident from his childhood. Devin didn't know how to tell her. It had now been decades since it occurred and the shame of it was a deep current within him, but he felt it was just that — a watercourse he had built his life around. Like a city that creates roads and buildings over springs and rivers and then let them run wild beneath the structures. But the waterway beneath Devin's life would soon swell and overrun his world.

"Alone in the Dark"
John Hiatt

At this point, he stopped. Up until that moment, as he told me the story, he just looked straight ahead at the lake and lands in the distance. Suddenly, he turned to me and spoke.

> "What happened just over a year ago?"

> "Wha...? Wait... to me?"

> "Yeah. What happened last winter?"

> "My wife and I separated."

> "Why?"

> "A lot of reasons... marriage is complicated."

> "It is. But something happened before that, at the Green Trust. It's where we began. But you still don't know why it happened, do you?"

> "What the hell? What are you doing?"

> "Okay. I'll tell you. Devin was brought in to write a strategic plan for one of Canada's largest and most successful environmental organizations—The Green Trust. He was recommended for the job as a consultant. The organization was rife with staff issues. The chief reason for these problems was the leader: Harry Cohen."

> "I have it right?"

> "So far."

> "Harry was the Executive Director. Those that recommended Devin to help get the organization on-track were Harry's greatest critics. So, he was distrustful of Devin and adversarial when they met. Devin thought he had made

progress in his meetings with Harry to build some level of trust and common ground. He prided himself on this. And then Harry died a few days after their last meeting. Harry had left for Miami and died there from a massive heart attack.

Devin had to continue his work after the funeral. It was winter. Devin sat at the boardroom table. He was nervous. But about what? He couldn't figure out what was bothering him. He often found he was a little blue in the winter. So, he began thinking about summer plans. It was an old coping method he had for dealing with the darkness and cold of January and February. He would travel in his mind to memories of summers on lakes and rivers and make plans for the coming warmer months. He turned his mind back to lead the day's session on charting the future. And then he could hear a child's voice talking to him. "Did you eat all the jelly beans?"

There was his childhood friend, Sean. Walking across the bridge on the last day they were together.

Devin was shocked. His pulse rose. He began to sweat. He gripped his seat with white knuckles. His stomach turned. He knew what was coming, and he couldn't stop it. Sean was going to be hit by a car. He was about to die.

Devin looked at the ground. He thought he might throw up. He started to slide off the seat. He was pouring with sweat and panting. He closed his eyes and could only hear screams and screeching. He bolted from the room.

Devin ran to the bathroom. He was sick, and when he cleaned himself up he looked in the mirror. *Pale*, he thought. *As a ghost*. He tried to catch his breath. His phone was buzzing in his jacket pocket. He reached in to get it and found a bag of jelly beans.

One of the board members, Joseph, came into the bathroom. Devin said he was battling the flu.

Of course, the board understood this. Devin had a member of his team take the lead for the rest of the day."

He stopped and looked at me.

"Harry died because of a pre-existing condition. Not because of anyone. It wasn't anyone's fault. But Devin was gutted. He felt responsible. He had built a career where he could fix things with words and actions. Here, he decided that he failed and not only that, he had contributed to the death of a man. Right?"

He could tell his words were getting to me. I was fuming.

"Yes. Why would you do this?"

The anger in me subsided, and the sadness rose. I wept. Beneath the waxing moon, on top of a cliff, overlooking a great lake. I stood up and dove heedlessly into the lake thirty feet beneath us. I swam away from the island, from the man's voice, from everything I knew. I lay on my back in the water and stared into the universe. I tried to block out everything around me from my sight to only see the stars and sky. To be all alone in the dark. So I could feel like I was floating in space, so far away from everything.

"Hollow Man"
R.E.M.

After I swam for a while, I looked back to the cliff and saw
him point to a spot along the coast. He began walking to it,
and I made my way through the water to it. When we met, he
silently offered a hand, and he helped me out of the lake. He
turned and made his way back up the cliff.

"I suppose I should follow you."

"It's your choice. I told you that from the start."

"I'm not sure I like you."

"That's fine."

"You know, it's hard to have a fight with you?"

"I'm sure that's frustrating for you."

"It is."

"Should I continue?"

"I guess so. That's why I'm here."

—

The problem was that Devin couldn't trust himself not to have
this happen again. That night, he disappeared into a bar in
Toronto with bourbons, low light, and no questions. Five
doubles later he was wandering the streets. He had to stay out
late enough that both Mia and Lily would be asleep. He
couldn't face them. He arrived home around 1:30 a.m., turned
on a recorded episode of the Daily Show and fell asleep on the
couch.

The morning was rough. Lily woke him on the couch.
He held her and then watched her play with her toys.

He knew how to recover from a hangover but not this. He had never experienced anything like it before—a flashback he couldn't stop. Would it happen again? Next time, would he be driving his car with Lily in the back seat? The thought paralyzed him.

He watched her playing on the floor. He had found a box of his childhood toys that included a metal spinning top. It had a rod with a handle at the end, and when you pushed it down, the top would spin. The scenes of cartoon characters and the design details would blur and then form new shapes spinning in front of him. He watched her turn it. He became anxious and nauseous. Devin looked away.

He knew he needed to make significant changes in his life. But he didn't know how to speak to Mia about it. As he thought about how he could talk to her, he remembered when he almost told her before. They both loved going to the movies. They had come out of a film where a man recounted his childhood trauma with such raw emotion that it sent Devin spinning. As they walked out of the theatre, his head was swimming. They walked down an alley to get their car, and Devin stopped, bent over and began sobbing.

He was consumed by his reaction and had forgotten Mia was there. When he did, he could see an emotionless expression on her face. It shocked him, and he suddenly felt ridiculous and weak. He had never let anyone see him like this. And now that he did, he saw there was no comfort, only a perplexed expression. He pulled himself together and fell back into his silence. He couldn't risk telling her if that was her response. So, he went back to bed. Mia took Lily to daycare, and at lunch, he got a call from her.

"Are you okay?"

Without a thought, he blurted out a response. "I need to get out of the city, I need to go back home. Where I grew up. I just feel so miserable, and it's not getting better. I shouldn't feel this way. But I do. It's not your fault... All I know is I've got to go home."

Mia was surprised to find herself angry. "I knew this was coming. You've been so restless, so unhappy."

"I'm sorry I didn't know that it was so obvious."

"It was."

"If you knew it was coming, why didn't you do anything about it? Why didn't you say something?"

"I just assumed I would lose you one day. And that would be that."

"That would be that? I have to go."

From that night on, he never slept in their home again. He arranged time with Lily. A friend of a friend had a furnished apartment that was available for rent, so he moved into it. He wanted to live alone.

—

My storyteller paused.

"If you could talk to her today, what would you say to her?"

"Damn it. Okay. If I'm honest, I would say that it must have been painful to love me, live with me, and see me grow increasingly unhappy. How could she trust our relationship? How could she not feel it was her, at least, partially causing this? Of course, it wasn't. I would say I'm sorry I kept you at bay. I wanted to be more than what I felt I was. To admit that I was part of this accident and the shame I felt for it was too much for me. But I know that was not fair to you. As my partner, I owed it to you to share this with you, but I wasn't ready. All of this has left me feeling like a shell of a man, hollow and uneasy. You married only a portion of me. I'm incomplete. You deserve more, and I can't be what I know you want. So, I'm trying to figure out how to repair myself to be a decent father, and hopefully, a friend to you. I do wonder if we chose each other because we both keep others at a distance. Maybe that was the unsaid pact between us... I need to break it."

The sun was climbing behind us. Dawn was arriving raw and enchanting.

He seemed satisfied with me.

"I suppose we should go back now."

"Gimme a few minutes."

One thought kept surfacing, and I would try to push it back down only to have it resurface. *I need to talk. I need to quit living as a man broken into pieces, running off in all directions.* I knew that I had a decision to make. Would I just sit back and listen to what had happened in the past, or would I step into my story? Would I finally take part in my own life? If there was ever a time to do so, it was now.

I needed to take over the story from our narrator. *I* needed to author what would happen next.

"Shooting Star"
Bob Dylan

The summer sun was burning off the dew, the world was waking with its small, intimate noises and stirrings.

Devin tried to recall when he last greeted the dawn in the country.

In high school. Tired but alive. I know what I have to do, but I didn't know how to broach it with Alexander. I'll just state it plainly.

"I need to go back there. I need to drive down those streets."

Alexander stiffened. "Right. You need to go back there. You're ready?"

"Yes."

"When do you want to go?"

"Whenever you're ready."

"What's it like in Scott's Mills now?"

"The same."

"You've been back?"

"Yup."

"To the bridge?"

"Yeah."

"What do you do?"

"I stand on that road and scream."

With that, Alexander turned away from the scene and began walking towards his house. Devin followed him.

As they drove to the ferry, Devin's anxiety grew. He hadn't been back to the site of the accident since the summer it happened. The thought of returning made his stomach turn. He had a headache. He also couldn't stop himself from thinking about the series of circumstances that led him here. And he was surprised to find it made him angry.

Why, if there is some sort of God or reason to things, was I made to witness this cruel death? And all I could do was see it. I couldn't stop it. To only witness it seems cruel. Maybe this needed to happen to me. To make me more empathetic. If I look at the line of men who came before me, I see how they were compelled to participate in violence. My father worked in law enforcement and intelligence. My grandfather served every year of World War Two in battle. Nearly six years. He refused to go home and leave his men behind. Maybe my task is to deal with the trauma for all of us. Both of those generations of men were taught to suffer in silence and isolation. There was no healing for them. We asked so much of them and offer so little in return. Not even a balm for the wounds they suffer.

This day also bred Alexander. I always accepted that Alexander was strong and that I was weak. But I sense that Alexander needs me now as much as I had needed him in the past. He has been living the same life for almost twenty years. He doesn't seem happy. He's alone. Maybe this growing humanity is my true strength and my gift to Alexander, my father, and other men. My ability to feel compassion towards all, and to articulate that. Maybe his strength allowed me to be what he always wanted me to be…

The thought made him feel strong… for the first time.

They arrived at the bridge. Alexander hopped out of the car before it even stopped and began to walk to the steep path that would lead to the area beneath the bridge where he'd begun. Devin stopped the car and saw where Alexander was going. He jumped out and shouted at him.

"Alexander. Stop."

Alexander turned around, surprised.

"Come with me."

Alexander enjoyed the sudden assertiveness in Devin. He turned back from the trail to join Devin on the bridge. They stood together. A few cars went by.

"This is where it happened that day, Alexander."

"Yes, it is," he said quietly, in return.

"Thank you for being with me all of these years. I might not have come out from under there if you hadn't pulled me out. I don't know if I would've made it without you."

Tears were forming in Devin's eyes as he spoke.

"Thank you."

Devin reached out and put his arms around Alexander. Alexander remained silent.

He whispered as he held him: "Alex, only one of us is getting back into that car."

Alexander nodded, stepped back and punched Devin in the face. Blood spurted from his nose. He lifted his hand to it as he fell to his knees, and Devin felt that it was bent to the left. Likely broken.

"Damn you," he moaned.

"Damn you, too," Alexander responded with a smile.

Alexander reached out his hand to help Devin off the ground. Devin had started to rise on his own, and pushed Alexander's hand away.

"Good," he replied.

Alexander grabbed him. Devin responded. Their arms intertwined. Devin was angry. Foreheads crashed. They careened across the bridge and tumbled down the hill. They stood and grappled with each other until they were under the bridge. Devin threw Alexander and pinned him to the ground. Alexander relented. He smiled.

He looked down at Alexander and sighed. He placed a hand on Alexander's chest. "Alexander," he said slowly. There was no anger now.

Alexander looked up at him. "You're okay, then? You'll be okay?"

Devin nodded. Alexander punched him again, on the side of the head, rendering him unconscious.

A wind kicked up, and when Devin gained consciousness a few moments later, he was alone.

"River"
Leon Bridges

I am no longer Devin or Alexander. I am just one person. I am the narrator. You may not like him much, but I feel honest in the world and open for the first time in my memory. I'm not at ease or content, but I'm honest about it. There is no mask.

I hope you can understand why I needed to tell the story this way. There is no way out, but through, I suppose. I fell into this hole years ago, and only I could jump into it to pull myself out.

The day Sean died, I ran from the accident, and I've been running ever since. I'm slowing to a stop now. I ran from the pain and sorrow, and I gained speed and kept running. I even ran from Sean. I made no room for the memory of my friend in my life. And I needed to start there. I needed to just let the memory live with me.

The details of the accident were hard to piece together. My mind fought me when I tried to access them. I've read that it's a self-defense mechanism. So, I forced myself to stay in a chair and stare out a window. I watched the gentle swaying of an elm in the light winds to lull my mind to rest. Once it fell calm, I turned my thoughts to the accident. My brain tried to squirm away. And then it just refused my access to the memories. It crossed its arms, took a wide stance and refused to remember. I stood my ground and pushed past it to the event itself. I began to sweat. Sean was crawling to me, there was so much blood. I thought I was going to vomit. My heart broke open. I held him. I wept over him. I knew he was going to die. And he did die. I can't dress this up or be more artful about it. He died. I couldn't stop it, and maybe I contributed to his death. I had blood on my hands.

Tears streamed down my face. I gasped for air. The only words were, "Oh, Sean."

I wept for a long time alone in that chair with the trees swaying in the yard. And then a weight lifted with one thought.

It wasn't my fault. It was just an accident. I was just a kid.

I hadn't spoken about the accident for so long that old feelings of shame were allowed to stay without being challenged. For when they were, I realized, I was not responsible. No better or worse than any other child. We were just thrown into this experience. If I was going to deal with it, I had to spend time with all of the elements of the accident. And so, I began to divide my time between Toronto and Cashell Island.

The day my friend died, I knew two facts, and I had one question. First, I was an accomplice or co-conspirator in taking the bike. The second fact was that I had broken the rules. My mother had forbidden me to ride this bicycle that was clearly too big for us. I did it anyway, and my friend died. And that led to the most challenging question I have ever had to ask myself: *Why was I allowed to live?*

For decades now, these thoughts haunted me. I also never shared them with anyone. I lived in the half-light of that exiled land that we know as shame. This is what it feels like to have blood on your hands.

It's winter. A cold snap has arrived. Everything struggles against it. I'm pushed inside. It's such a deep chill that it hurts to be outside. I feel trapped.

I dreamt about the accident last night. A tire wheel. The terrible sounds, and then the sight of Sean on the pavement, and I can't help him. I was useless. I let him down. I wake up terrified and then remember and just feel exhausted, despairing. I went to see my doctor, who sent me to a psychologist. I was resistant, but I knew I didn't want to live as I had been for years. I had a hard time imagining that seeing a doctor could make it worse.

The windowless room of her office felt like a cage or a prison. I fidgeted in my chair as she prepared her notebook.

"So, why are you here?"

"I guess it's the slightly better of two bad choices."

"And what are they?"

"I can't wait to have another... incident, where I live out a flashback from an accident, or where I try to deal with it."

"Why is trying to deal with it such a terrible thing?"

"Because there is no 'dealing with it'. It happened. I couldn't stop it then, and I can't stop it now. There's nothing to deal with — I'm just reliving it here with you, or I can let it come on its own accord, not see it coming, and I can let it knock me down."

I didn't realize how angry I was about this. As I paused, I realized I was taking it out on her. It was unfair. She sat silently.

"Okay. I'm sorry. I'm not mad at you. I just don't know what to do."

"I can tell. You can't sit still. It's like you bounce off subjects and the world around you."

She was right. I went silent.

"I don't feel relaxed. I rarely do. That's true."

"Why do you think that is?"

Okay, I thought. *I'm here. If I'm going to do this. I need to do this now.*

"We shouldn't have been on the bike that day. I got off, and he died. Why? Why do I get to live, and he has to die? Why? It was thirty years ago, and I feel the same way. Why? I've rarely told anyone about this. I've let snippets of this out when I was drunk with a couple of close friends, but that's it. I feel ashamed. And then I feel crazy for feeling ashamed. And I just want to walk away from it all, but I can't. I owe Sean more than that. So, I spend my life helping others. I've made a living trying to stand up for others and by fixing everything around me. I'm worn out from it, and the need doesn't seem to go away. Lately, it doesn't even bring me any satisfaction... So... Do you regret asking me?"

After I uttered the last line, I realized I was crying. I've never wept about this with someone else present. I put my head in my hands.

When I left her office that day, I felt lighter. Unburdened. Like I had removed a backpack of stones. And I looked forward to seeing her in a week.

"Cyprus Avenue"
Van Morrison

After seeing the psychologist for a few months, I started to feel stronger and more at ease. And I wanted to fully understand the accident and talk to those involved in it and those that were close to Sean. I needed to see them. I can't explain why or what I would say, but I wanted to speak to them. Like all half-baked plans, this could only go well.

There was nothing online about it. So, I travelled to the Scott's Mills archives. Being a small village, Scott's Mills' records were in the public library in the nearby, larger town of Trenton.

I was five at the time, so that would have meant it occurred in 1977. I searched the papers for May and June 1977 and found no mention of the crash. I searched again, from April to July. Nothing. Had I imagined it? I was sweating. My pulse rose. I had to keep my calm. Volunteers from the library were near me, helping another person. A woman was researching her genealogy. I wished my search was less desperate, more enjoyable. I sat back in my chair. Had I gone crazy? There was turmoil in my childhood outside of this event. My mother struggled with depression, my father was often away, and there were fights when he came home. We also moved frequently. I went to five schools in eight years. And then, the divorce. There was constant upheaval. Maybe I invented Sean and his death as a way to cope with my own mental anguish? Perhaps it gave me a single, external cause for my restlessness, anger, and shame. Had I just inherited mental health problems and created this incident in my mind? I slumped in my chair. I was trying to catch my breath.

I pulled myself together and did the math again. It was the end of kindergarten. You're five in kindergarten. But it was in June, at the end of the school year. The school year started in September 1977, but it ended in June of 1978. I rushed over to the metal unit with drawers that held the films of old newspapers. The Trentonian came out twice a week. I

143

sped through the months of 1978 until I got to June. I searched through the weekly papers. I found it. I sighed and then, of course, felt pangs of sorrow and waves of pain. It was true. The tragedy did occur. Sean was dead.

I leaned back, conquered in my seat, and cried tears into the dust of this public space and its facts. If I'm honest, I know I would have chosen madness over the truth.

My friend only had one chance to be on the cover of the newspaper. The details of it made it all seem so familiar, so minor. He "swung into a lane of traffic and was struck by a bumper." "Swung" is so playful. And I guess we were playing at the time. A "bumper" also sounds playful. I thought the job of the bumper was to soften the blow. I was wrong. Researching the device, I found that "bumpers offer protection to other vehicle components by dissipating the kinetic energy generated by an impact..." Nowhere is a person noted. Nowhere did they consider Sean. Just the parts of the car.

He was actually mentioned in two front-page stories. The second was titled "Black Week In Quinte." "Five people died in accidents within a three-day period..." Our parents were so young. On my side, at times, five generations were living. Children begetting children. About every twenty years, a firstborn.

My parents were still in their twenties. My paternal grandfather had taken his own life two years before Sean passed away. My grandfather was severely injured at the end of the war. His jeep hit a landmine, I believe. His body was no longer just his own. It became home to plates and pins meant to piece him together, and drugs to keep the pain at bay. But nothing could help the nightmares, and the pain never ceased. He would awake screaming, and the pain would surge in him. One day, he'd had enough. He took his pain medication, a blanket, and walked down to the Napanee River. He lay down to rest beside the water and with a dignified swallowing of too many pills, never rose again.

I, of course, was too young to know any of this at the time. But for my father, it must have been devastating. My dad did what many of the men of his time would have done: he kept his chin up. Then, he would sit alone in his pain, or distance himself from others to nurse his sorrows. And I can only imagine what he felt losing his father to suicide when he was only twenty-four. He has never openly spoken to me about it. I don't push him because as much I would like to know more, he was his father. Like him, I had learned from an early age that a man suffers silently, alone.

Sean's parents dealt with the inverse tragedy. The parents of all young children who die must live with one of the greatest fractures a person can endure: the death of your child. That death is always tragic. Even if it's a disease, it's devastating because we've lost something we should not have lost. When that happens, we have to wonder, as a community, where we went wrong.

As I sat with the printouts of newspaper articles and genealogical records, I began to see it clearly. In the wound, there is more than an ache. In witnessing a sudden death at a young age, I had found the sanctity of life and a deep abiding compassion towards others. I now had Sean's obituary, his parents' and siblings' names, and the name of the driver of the vehicle that day. And that now haunted me. What struck me with tremendous force was the details about the driver. Diana. She was only eighteen. What a way to leave high school and enter adulthood—saddled with having killed a child! I wanted to find her, to tell her that it wasn't her fault, that she needed to forgive herself for this, if she hadn't already done so. I imagined the burden she carried from that day.

I was also compelled to find Sean's family. They had to know how much he mattered to me. It wasn't for nothing, his death. It tortured me but also pushed me forward in life.

This may sound strange, but having these names and these artifacts from the accident gave me comfort. It brought to surface the terrible details, but it also let me know that I, finally, wasn't alone in it. There was a community of people now. I could relieve myself of isolation.

The first person I needed to see was Sean. It was a short drive from Trenton to the cemetery. It was less than fifty kilometers from Sean's childhood home. It was comforting to know that he was close to where his family lived. But I also thought that he probably never travelled much farther than this in his entire life. There was so much he didn't see and that he never experienced. A first kiss, travelling on an airplane to a new place, having kids of his own... I crossed the short distance to him with purpose, but a heaviness sat on my chest.

The cemetery sat on a hill surrounded by woods. I parked near the entrance and walked the grounds, searching for his grave marker. It was surrounded by statues of cherubs. I only managed to utter one line: "I'm sorry it took me so long to come and see you." Then I wept.

Once I had collected myself, I placed some flowers beside the stone and then I talked to him a bit about my life. "A lot has happened. I'm less into mud pies these days, for example..." As I said goodbye, I told him that I would be back. "I miss you, my friend, and I'll come back to see you. Let's celebrate your life. I will be back for your birthday each year. I'm so happy you were born, and we were friends. I want to celebrate that each year... And it's not just because I won't have to share the cake."

"Astral Weeks"
Van Morrison

As much as I felt better visiting Sean's grave, I still felt anger and sadness.

I was left with troubling questions. Whose fault was this accident? Where the hell were our parents? Why didn't they stop him from riding the bike? Why were we going to school alone at the age of six?

As I spoke to friends about this, I realized that this was the case for most people. Our parents had to work. Our mothers were trying to find a place in the world. Mine was, for sure. It was a struggle for her. We relied on her contributions, along with my dad's. And my parents, like others, trusted that the community would keep us safe. The more I thought about it, the more I realized that this also made my generation independent, self-reliant.

I sat with this notion for a long time until I heard a voice whispering to me, "Your mother forbid you from riding his bike to school. So, you had to get off the bike near the bank where she worked. It was because you weren't on the bicycle that you survived." It's because my mother was trying to help me, and because I had listened to her that I survived. Sure, the day could have gone differently if we were both not on bikes, and maybe the truck would have missed. But maybe not. Regardless, I survived that day, and I listened to my mother. I survived. For some thirty years, I had never thought of this.

I knew I had to talk to people about the accident. I owed it to my family to start with them.

I sat with my mother and spoke a little, looking for an opening to discuss the accident. It didn't appear. So, I just announced it. She grew silent. I'm sure that it was terrible to think of her son amid this violence and loss. So close to dying. But I knew I had to talk about it. And I wanted to comfort her.

"Mom, I may not have survived if it hadn't been for you. Thank you."

She began to cry.

"I'm okay," I told her. You did nothing wrong. In fact, you may have saved me."

I held her.

"Why do you think I've been so strange for so long?"

"What do you mean?"

"I've never told anyone about this. I've been nothin' but a stranger in this world for too long."

Driving home, I thought, maybe this is all there is. We're moving through this space and time, and the best we can do is help each other through it. The best moments are that — just helping someone through it.

The living needed more from me than I had offered so far.

PART III

"Wait"
Alexi Murdoch

It's been almost two years since Mia and I broke up. I have a new place in Toronto for Lily and me by the lake. The highlight of each day is the time after dinner. Lily puts on her pajamas, and we cross our street to climb on the boulders on the beach along the edge of the sand. Eventually, she will ask to climb onto my lap and look out at the great lake in silence. I love that moment, that it's her idea, and the way her tiny body relaxes and leans back into mine, against my chest. I kiss the top of her head, and enjoy the moment.

Recently, my friends, Sinead and her husband, Malcolm, hosted a dinner party to introduce me to a friend of theirs. They had done this without telling either of us. When this woman, May, entered the room, she immediately caught my attention. I found myself distracted all evening, thinking of her and trying to engage her without trying too hard. She was self-possessed, intelligent, kind, and stunningly beautiful.

I was nervous and unsure. I never learned how to be at ease with being attracted to someone and slowly getting to know them. Instead, I would pursue them, and once an intimacy was established, I was gone.

At the age of twenty, I started to date Katherine. She was studying dance at our university. We quickly fell for each other. We were on a date at the Queen Mother Cafe in Toronto. I adored her. She began to ask more about me, and I felt the familiar pain and darkness creeping in. She wanted to get closer to me. Everything in me recoiled. I had to look away, so my eyes found the top of the MuchMusic building across the street. One red light stood on top of a signal tower in the darkness of the Toronto night. The gloom was deep and wide.

It was all I could look at. And then the loneliness of that light. So small, finite, meaningless. I knew that darkness had spread across me like spilt oil in a parking lot. Leaving it stained. Even then, even in this blissful state of comfort, of caring, it was there. I had no idea what to do but to carry it. And I decided I needed to do that alone. It was all I knew to do.

So, I grew silent. I ended the date early. Katherine tried to talk to me, but I was rude and cold. She left in tears. And I let her feel that way. I offered her nothing. Then I sat alone drinking in a bar. Katherine was one more person thwarted trying to travel the distance to me. She meant me no harm and, like others, would be left unsure of what happened other than we spent time together and then I was gone.

I felt guilty for this and dived deeper into drinking, winding up on the rooftop of a friend's place downtown, drunk, performing an acrobatic walk along the ledge of the building, twenty stories high. Madness.

So, I decided I wouldn't do this anymore. I wouldn't listen to that part of myself that wanted to run. I didn't need to be alone anymore.

I tried to speak to May a few times at the party. Unlike me, she was aware that something was afoot. She was being set up. Each time I spoke to her, she felt like all eyes turned to her. And it made her grow silent. I didn't know this. So, after three attempts to have a conversation, I stopped. Maybe she just wasn't interested in me. Sensed I was a single dad in therapy, dealing with post-traumatic stress disorder. Her apparent apprehension showed good judgment. I trusted a woman who was ambivalent about me. So, I went to the living room and wrestled with Lily and the other kids.

Fortunately, I was wrong about May's skepticism towards me. I was happy to get an email a couple of days after the party from Sinead filling me in that May would be interested in meeting me again. I was nervous, but I agreed.

After one of our initial dates, we went for a stroll along the boardwalk in front of my house. We stopped and sat on a bench. She leaned back into me while quietly staring out to the lake. I could feel my panic rising.

No, stay here. Sit here, perfectly still, and wait for it to pass.

So, I told her everything. I was open and honest, for the first time, about my past. I was shocked and comforted at her ease with it. As I stepped back and considered what I was telling her, I became aware that no one would judge me for that day. It was never my fault. The greatest judge about this was me. Maybe I was always the only judge.

I fell in love with May. For the first time, I let her do the same. I let her fall in love with all of me. Of course she saw my kindness, and there was a bit of a brain at work, some strength, but also the simmering pot of anger and sorrow that I was trying to take off the stove.

She had her struggles, and my open admission about my own let her share them. It allowed her to be close to me, and maybe, a little freer.

"Save Me"
Aimee Man

I found Anna on Facebook.

The day after going to the library and visiting Sean's grave, I searched for the names mentioned in the obituary. I found a couple, including Sean's older sister. I was sure I found Anna on the social media site. It was the same name, she was living in the same area, and I recognized her face in the profile picture. So, I decided to send her a message. I struggled with the language. I resolved to confirm it was her and then ask her to meet me. At least, that was my plan.

Devin
Hi Anna, I think you lived across the road from me in Scott's Mills when we were kids, right?

Anna
Hi Devin, I'm not sure, but maybe—I did live in Scott's Mills.

Devin
Yeah, you had a brother and a sister? On Oxford Street.

Anna
Yup.

Devin
This may sound strange, but I was hoping I could meet you sometime. I wanted to talk to you...

Anna
About?

(I struggled with this. I didn't want to tell her who I was online. It seemed such a cheap way to do it. On the other hand, if she didn't remember me, I was just some stranger asking to meet her, and I imagined that would seem more than strange—dangerous for her. So, I decided to deal with it directly. I had to tell her.)

Devin
It's personal. I'd prefer not to talk about it here. I understand if that makes you feel uncomfortable, and I can give you more info if this seems too strange.

Anna
This does seem strange to me. Sorry.

(Okay, here I go, I thought. She deserves to know why I want to meet with her...)

Devin
No need to apologize. I understand. It's about Sean. I was with him the day he passed away.

Anna
Oh, wow.

Devin
I'm so sorry to spring this on you.

Anna
Are you the one that ran to the house and told my dad?

Devin
Yeah.

Anna
I can't imagine how scared you must have been.

Devin
We were so young.

Anna
I've thought about you often.

Devin
I want you and your family to know it's been with me my whole life. Sometimes it's been really hard, but it's also made me want to lead a good life...

(I stopped here because I was sobbing. There was a long pause before Anna responded. I worried that I had said too much.)

Anna
Sorry, I had to walk away from my phone for a minute — this is a little overwhelming.

Devin
I'm sorry to overwhelm you.

Anna
It's just taken me by surprise. But don't be sorry.

Devin
Maybe we can meet sometime?

Anna
Yeah, I would like to meet to talk more.

We exchanged contact information, and a few months later, we had arranged to meet at her house. It took her that time, I assume, to gather the strength to see me, knowing it would bring up difficult memories.

May had asked if I wanted her to go with me to see Anna. I didn't know what I wanted. There was no precedent for this sort of encounter. I didn't know what to do. Part of me knew I was comfortable going alone. Because this is what I'd always known. When things were difficult, I would go it alone. But today, I wouldn't. I needed to quit hiding this. I asked May to join me. I was no longer on the move from one thing to the next with few connections. I was in my life. I wasn't running away from anything. I was no longer embracing evacuation and exile.

As May and I drove to Anna's home, I felt restless and nervous. May tried to ask me how I was doing. I replied with a clipped "fine." She allowed me the space to be distracted. I was unprepared, but how could I be prepared? I hadn't thought about what I would say. I didn't realize that until I was in Anna's driveway about to get out of the car. I now wanted time to compose myself, but I knew that I only had a few minutes before it would become strange. She knew I was coming, at this time, and she likely saw me in her driveway.

She opened the door and stepped back. There was a faint smile. I felt like I was a sort of invader. I was on the landing, and it was a few steps up to the main floor where her husband was standing. He was in his early fifties, bald, and held a neutral expression on his face. I expected a typical, warm welcome, but was received with hesitation. I handed her a bottle of wine. I smiled broadly and spoke. "It's so nice to meet you in person. Thanks for taking the time."

"Yes, yes, of course... and thank you."

I forgot May was with me. "This is my partner, May."

They both smiled and nodded. May reached out her hand. She felt the tension between us and was unsure how to ease it.

"This is my husband, Paul."

He firmly shook my hand.

"Do you want some of the wine you brought," Anna offered. She was unsure and uneasy. I felt like I'd brought that feeling into their house.

"I think I might need it," I said, trying to add levity.

She poured the wine silently while her husband stood beside her. I stood at the edge of their kitchen, looking into their living room. May remained silent.

"Welcome," Anna said without a smile. "Sit down."

I fell into an expansive couch with lots of pillows near a bay window. May joined me. Anna sat on the loveseat nearby, and her husband settled into a chair beside the loveseat.

"Well, I thought it would be good for us to meet," I said.

"Yeah, I'm glad you reached out to me. I remember my dad talking about you. Talking about the little boy that came running to our house to tell him."

Any level of detail that included me in that day stirred me.

"I never knew who you were, but I thought about this little boy. When you reached out to me and told me you lived across the street, it jogged my memory. I remembered you and your sister and that you were Sean's friend."

"Oh, really?"

She nodded silently.

"I wanted you to know that it meant a great deal to know your brother. That it's been hard obviously dealing with being the person that was there with him, but — "

"Oh my God, you were there?" she blurted out.

It was the first splash of emotion that emerged from her, and the feelings and the reaction took me by surprise.

"Yeah... that's why I wanted to see you."

"I thought you just heard about it and came to tell us. I thought you came upon the accident..."

I was shocked. I just assumed they knew I was there. "No, I was there. I got off the bike. I wasn't supposed to be on it, and my mom worked at the bank, so when we got near the bank, I hopped off the bike and walked beside Sean. We went a little way, and he swerved into the street a little, and that was when the accident happened..."

"Oh, my God!" Paul said.

Anna began to tear up. May rubbed my back.

"What did your parents say to you?" she asked me.

"I never told them. I never spoke about it."

He spoke up again. "You never told them? You never told anyone?"

"No. I was ashamed."

Silence settled into the room.

My head was swimming, I felt like the room was moving, but I forced myself to speak. *You have your speech.* So, I gave them my speech.

"I wanted you to know that it mattered a lot to me. He was my first best friend. And I have had to struggle with this, but it also made me want to live a great life for both of us. I'm the first person in my family to graduate from university. I've worked to help a lot of charities and have helped a lot of great people get elected to help our communities..." I couldn't hold it together any longer and started to cry. "That's gotta mean something..." I bowed my head, gasped for air. I felt like a child.

I raised my head as I captured my breath. "I'm sorry, sometimes it's just hard."

She moved from her seat to sit beside me and embraced me. I accepted it but was overwhelmed. This was not what I had intended to do.

They clearly didn't seem to know what to do with me. What would they do with the man who witnessed the death? She had her own losses. I'm sure Anna's husband wanted to ensure she could handle this. I was a stranger dropping salt water onto their sofa. I was a burden.

"I'm sorry... I should go."

She interrupted me and started talking about her family. Her father was doing okay and was living in a nearby nursing home. Her little sister, Alicia, struggled and sometimes lived with them. Doreen, her mother, had passed a few years ago.

"I always thought that the blessing is that she finally got to be with Sean."

Anna had children of her own that also lived nearby. She and her husband had decent jobs. He was an adult educator, and she was a senior salesperson in health care products. As she talked, my memory found her. She looked much the same as I remembered her before I moved away. She amazed me. There was a constant river of patience and love that ran within her. She was like the spring in the nearby town of Tagnewheta in the aptly named Springside Park. I loved going there as a child. Everyone did. It was a constant offering of water that emerged from the earth in a tiny cave. Like Anna, it flowed from some unseen source. It attracted others to it, and they fed on it and marveled at the mystery of this generous, constant outpouring.

She finally asked me if I had "seen" Sean since the accident. She told me that he had come to her after the crash and a few more times.

"It was always the same—in my bedroom, his arms outstretched to me. I would hold him," she said and began to weep. "I would hold him as long as he would let me. I didn't know what else to do for him." I held her while she cried.

Silences grew. I had said all I could say, and so had Anna. We had given as much as we could. We needed a respite now.

As I started to leave and we said our goodbyes, she kept chatting with me. They told me that we should see each other again. May agreed. I put on my shoes feeling lost, weak, and useless. I realized I hadn't brought her good news like I had tried to make myself believe I would. If I was honest with myself, I would admit that I hadn't gone there to tell her that her brother's death held meaning. I had gone there to confess, and I was seeking my own forgiveness. I was hiding that from myself. She had lost her brother, and I wanted her to make me feel better? I wanted anyone to save me. What a selfish thing to do.

I also knew she had shown me love. She knew it was all I needed.

I had lost some of my shame, but it was like losing your only pair of shoes that also give you blisters. Now you just didn't have shoes. Now you had a new problem. May could tell I was sinking. She held my hand. She kissed my cheek. I was immune. I sped down their driveway. I didn't want to speak. I just told May that I wanted to stop at a nearby gas station. It also served as a liquor store, and I bought a pack of cigarettes and a mickey of whiskey. I walked outside and cracked open the bottle and lit a cigarette. Then I stopped. I tossed both the pack of cigarettes and the bottle in the garbage. I got into the car. May had been watching me.

"Are you okay?" she asked.

"No," I said. She reached out and wrapped her arms around me.

"Do you think you could drive?" I asked. Tears were running down my face.

"Of course."

I got in the passenger seat, put on some music and sent Anna a text.

"Anna—thanks so much for taking the time to meet me. I hope you didn't find it too difficult. It was tough for me to see you, and I really appreciate the kindness you showed me. Thank you. I hadn't come to your home in search of that, but it was what I needed. Thank you, thank you, thank you. It means the world to me."

"Come Talk To Me"
Peter Gabriel

I slept soundly that night and rose with a single thought in my head: I need to tell this story. I had resisted my own tale because it was filled with grief. If each of us had a capacity for pain and sorrow, then forces beyond my control had poured a high volume of it into the cup of my life. I had been trying to manage a spilling mug of grief since I was six. Carrying that grief alone and then taking on the other pains I met meant I was walking wounded all the time.

There is a hardness in the centre of this. It's the uncooked kernel in a handful of popcorn you pull from the bowl. You sense it with your tongue and make sure you don't bite down. You spit it out. I was getting better. I felt calm, present, renewed. But no matter how much time passed, no matter how much we may massage it or let this rest, part of it will remain a hard substance that we will only break against. This death will always be a tragedy. So, no matter how much a sense of purpose, light, or most importantly, love comes from this; there will always be a hard centre of the tragedy that will stand through the years.

I was learning that the key was not to break upon that unyielding stone, but instead to let it be. To come up against it is to come up against the part of life we want to ignore — death. It's gut-wrenching and inevitable, but without it nothing else would matter. This life is only precious because it's precarious. Each day matters as we only have a limited number of them. Our joys and love and laughter are so meaningful in defiance of it. So, I will, at times, let myself cry. I will lie down with my sorrow when I must, but then I will get up. I won't let it wrestle me to the ground and keep me there, and I won't let myself live moping or be a paleness or scarcity.

If I'm honest, I realize that I've been carrying a secret for years, and no response is equal to the emotional weight of sharing your greatest shame and tragedy.

I owed it to my parents and the rest of my family to talk about the accident. I also owed it to myself. I needed to step out of the silence and have the people around me know this. I needed to be seen even if that meant I looked weak, foolish or culpable. I needed to be heard. It was the only way to unblock this misery.

Of all the conversations I had about this, I remember my father's words: "We just didn't know what to do about it." That was honest, vulnerable. And to utter those words required courage.

He may not have known I was with Sean, but he knew he was my best friend. I know he and my mother would have wanted to help me, but there were no tools given to them. I'm not sure how many parents at that time and place would have known how to handle this situation.

I also think of my dad's career. When I became an adult, I learned that his work involved much violence and trauma. He has rarely spoken to me about it. And I imagine that must carry weight. Is it fair what we ask people like him to shoulder? He has rarely spoken openly about the violence, or about the anxiety, and depression. All of this, and more, was his burden alone. And there's no meaningful support for those in this vocation. So, they learn coping mechanisms. Booze, drugs, sex. This way of being for men gets passed on from generation to generation. From those early moments of fear or of injury in the schoolyard, we're taught to suck it up, bear the damage and stifle the feelings, not speak about them and carry on silently. My role has been lonely because the burden I was given at an early age was more significant than most, but I know that my way of dealing with the pains of life was not unique to me. As men, this is what we're all taught.

If I'm honest, I will go back even further to the day when I was just a toddler and pulled out the black plastic tube to the washing machine that fed the hot water to the device. I scalded my neck and chest—third-degree burns. I have no memory, but the scar remains. This incident and the death of Sean are a lot for a child under six. They set me on a course with trauma. Like most men, I became alienated, frustrated, depressed, and angry. Being a wounded man is not unique. It's just the nature of my wound that is unique. The model we're asked to aspire to is that of the emotionless brute. When emotions escape us, they have the tenor of the overwrought tantrums of a child.

But I found meaning in sitting with the wounds. I learned to talk about them without reliving them. It seems we've become a culture of people who want to avoid sorrow, tragedy, and sadness. I know I did. I had to write this. But in writing this, I finally found the thing that needs to be written. I found my voice and most importantly for us, the living, I found myself in my own life. I wasn't running from myself. I wasn't battling or retreating. I wasn't coping. I wasn't acting out. I was sitting with the sorrows and tragedy I'd known and, at times, crying over them. And then I let them be.

"Ballerina"
Van Morrison

When I left Anna, she stood at the top of the stairs that led to the landing and stared at the door for some time. Her husband stayed behind her. Quietly. He stepped away, poured her another glass of wine and walked back to her. She turned to face him. There were tears on her cheeks. He wrapped his arms around her. She cried on his chest.

They revisited the night in a short conversation. He mostly listened to her. She was still in shock from so many things. Having someone there with his own experience brought it to life for her again. She was still shocked at the revelation that this man had not only been there with Sean, but was just here speaking about it now.

They prepared for bed. Anna felt a lightness after crying but was also tired. She was often tired after tears. She appreciated her husband's presence. But when they reached their bed, she wanted to lie alone and sink into sleep.

She wasn't sure how much time had passed, but she woke in her room. The moonlight shone through and lit it. She felt a presence, and looking around the room, she saw a figure in the doorway of the bedroom. It was a boy. She could see it was Sean. He reached out to her with both of his arms but said nothing. It had been many years since she had seen him, and the last time it was much like this. He was still a boy of six.

She opened her arms to him. "Sean," she said with lilting joy in her voice. He approached her. She was now sitting at the end of the bed. He wrapped his arms around her, and her head naturally fell onto his chest. He stroked her hair. She was so happy to hold him, and she gradually became aware that she was not holding him, but she was actually being held by him. She finally looked at him. His small tanned face and brown hair was just as she remembered them. He looked at her and quietly asked, "Okay?"

A new feeling arose in her. Sean was visiting her not to be comforted but to offer her comfort. He wanted to make sure he could leave her now. He wanted to say goodbye to her. "You've been trying to say goodbye for years, haven't you?" She wept and said, "Goodbye, my brother." Sean disappeared. She crawled over to her spot on the bed, slipped back beneath the blanket and sheets, then wrapped her body around her husband and fell asleep.

Hours later, Anna woke with a start. It was not because of noise but because she was filled with a surge of energy. She felt strangely invigorated. Different. She sat up in her bed and looked at the clock beside her: 6:24 a.m. It was still early. Her body felt odd—lighter and stronger. There were no aches or pains. She stepped lightly to their ensuite bathroom, closed the door, and looked in the mirror. It struck her immediately. She was younger now. In fact, it took her a few seconds to recognize herself. The lines around her eyes that she had for thirty or so years now were gone, and her eyes were less sunken. There were also no marks on her face or neck. Her skin was smooth, even. She touched it and felt like she had received a facial treatment. She liked the way she looked and loved the way she felt this morning.

She walked out into the hallway and had an intense desire to do the splits. She hadn't tried this for years. She did so in the middle of the kitchen, slowly and then quickly reaching the position. Smiling at how limber and firm her body was this morning, she broke into a laugh. It started as a low, inward laugh that grew until her husband came into the kitchen to find her there, her body spread across the kitchen floor, roaring loudly.

"Beside You"
Van Morrison

A day or two after being at Anna's, my thoughts turned to Diana. I still needed to find her. The notion that the girl — now a woman — was carrying this burden compelled me. I know what it's like to shoulder a burden. If I could find her, neither of us would have to be alone in dealing with this anymore. Maybe I could help her? Her story mattered.

As a man now twice the age she was at the time of the accident, all I could think was that she must have felt so guilty for so long. Did anyone tell her it was an accident? Did she know it was not her fault but a terrible set of circumstances? I bet no one told her the bike was too big for Sean and me. She needed to know those things. I was overcome with guilt for not looking for her before now. Because I had avoided dealing with this for so many years, I had, in turn, forced her to carry this on her own. Sean couldn't talk to her. Only I could. *I'll stand beside you, Diana,* I thought to myself.

Finding Sean's family was simple enough with social media. When I found the news reports of the accident, I also found   Diana's   name.

It's strange. I felt as though time was slipping away and I need to find Diana right away.

"Adagio for Strings"
Samuel Barber

Diana was in a rush. Being both tall and athletic, she could command space and efficiently move through the throng of her fellow students.

She had to get from her high school to the equestrian centre north of Belleville, and then back to high school before her next exam. She accidentally left the equestrian centre without her riding crop the night before. Her parents were adamant that she learned to be more responsible, so she was given the loan of her father's truck for school that day to return the riding crop. With no time for lunch, she sped through the halls to the parking lot.

Her best friend, Francine, caught sight of her rushing through the halls.

"D! Lunch?"

She barely slowed to tell her, "I can't. I gotta run to the barns. I forgot something. Or else my dad will kill me." The last line was delivered over her shoulder.

"Here!" said Francine. "You gotta eat something," and tossed a bag of jelly beans she had been snacking on between classes and was carrying now. Others turned to watch the pass. Many of them admired Diana. She had thick and shining blonde hair, alabaster skin, and strength and kindness that she shared generously. She was a natural leader in the minds of teachers and students alike.

"Thanks!" Diana hollered on her way out the door.

Cars could be travelling for an hour on this paved road through the countryside with no villages, lights or stop signs before reaching Scott's Mills. It seemed to have been dropped onto the highway. The stoplight would be the first time she had to slow down.

She saw the two boys a few blocks ahead of her. One was walking on the sidewalk, and the other was riding a bike that was clearly too big for him along the edge of the sidewalk. She moved through the intersection without having to break. Travelling a little faster than the speed limit. In her head, she gave thanks for the green light.

She didn't know why the boy on the bike swerved, but he did. She barely even had time to process it. Then there was that terrible sound.

She braked hard, and the truck screeched to a stop. She first saw the boy on the sidewalk. He was stunned. He was staring at the other boy on the road. He then started running towards the child on the ground. She could see that he was still conscious and trying to get up, and his friend was trying to help him. Her stomach turned as she reached them. The boy on the ground was bleeding from his mouth and nose, and his legs didn't work, so he was trying to pull himself up with his arms. He collapsed. He was unconscious and continued bleeding.

He was so small, she thought. Only five or six. She began to panic. His colour was changing, his breathing was laboured and shallow. The boy was holding his friend and talking to him, comforting him. When she arrived, he snapped out of it and turned to her.

"I'm going to get his dad. I'll go... I'll go and get his dad," he stammered.

As he ran down the street, cars began to stop at the site, and people surrounded the girl and the boy on the pavement. He was shivering. She ran to a nearby house to get blankets. When she came back, she instinctively held the boy in her arms. His body was twitching and bleeding. His eyes were closed. All she could do was wait. As others came near, she wept and asked for an ambulance. She held the boy's head in her lap, crying and whispered to him. "It's okay, it's okay." But of course, it wasn't. The boy did not reply.

"Winter"
Tori Amos

Things only got worse.

I can feel him slipping away. His body is lighter. Oh, my God. What do I do? I don't want to vomit. Swallow it. I don't understand. Why is everything so bright? I can't hear anything. It's getting hard to hear his breathing. It's like everything is light. I can't tell one thing from the next.

The police were kind to her when they arrived with the ambulance. They helped her up, while Sean was placed on a stretcher, unconscious. They asked her questions and put her in the back of their car and drove her to the hospital behind the ambulance. She sat motionless for the drive. Halfway there, they had to stop so she could step out of the vehicle and vomit on the side of the road.

"Is he gonna be okay?"

"I don't know."

"Will you take me to the hospital?"

"I should take you to the station."

"I wanna go to the hospital."

He sighed.

"Are you gonna take me to the hospital?"

"Okay."

In the hospital waiting room, one of the police officers asked her a few questions. She answered them as best she could about what happened, where she lived, and her name.

It seemed like they kept asking her the same questions over and over again until finally, she lost her temper.

"I told you! I told you! Just tell me if the little boy is gonna be okay!" She was furious. "I don't even know his name!" She wept after screaming. The police officer took her by the arm and sat down with her. He held her hand and just said one thing: "His name was Sean."

"Was?" She couldn't speak any more about it. She burst into a new round of tears.

"He died on the way to the hospital," the officer added gently.

Diana didn't know what to do next. She had just turned eighteen, so she was an adult, and her parents weren't called. She assumed they would come to the hospital, so she sat waiting for them under the fluorescent lights and on the vinyl seats in the hospital waiting room. She didn't wait long. It was only another ten minutes before one of the officers, Frank Jenkins, said he would take her home. He had heard that Sean's parents were on the way to the hospital. He didn't want them to run into this girl. He could interview her at her home.

Diana spoke very little in the car on the way there. She was looking through the window away from Frank. He could imagine her face. So sad. There were no words to tell her. He knew she would just keep staring towards something no one could see. She gave him directions to her parents' home in absent tones. When they arrived at the top of their driveway, he announced: "I'll come in with you."

"What... Why?"

"I'll tell them what happened."

There was a long pause. "Okay," she said.

It was now the middle of the afternoon, and only Diana's mother, Lillian, was home. She was shocked to hear the door open and steps in the foyer.

"Diana?"

The three of them sat at the kitchen table while Officer Jenkins explained the details of the accident to Lillian. Diana felt like she was hearing his story for the first time. A story that involved other people and carried terrible news. She felt terrible for all of them.

As Officer Jenkins explained it, he had Diana fill in the details: "Yes, I was southbound... He was on his bike on the street...Yes, he hit the passenger side." And then she broke down crying.

"I need to call my husband," Lillian interjected. Lillian called her husband. She spoke in hushed tones. Her voice went from quiet and somewhat calm to perplexed and annoyed. She moved and spoke slower now. She turned to the officer.

"I need to wash my daughter."

Diana's mother seemed suddenly tense, and this caught Officer Jenkins' attention. Diana looked at herself and saw blood on her thighs and shorts and a little on her right hand.

"Okay," she said.

Officer Jenkins nodded but remained seated.

Halfway up the sweeping staircase in the foyer, Diana turned to her mother and stopped. "Mom... I didn't get the riding crop," and again broke down in tears.

They made their way to the bathroom, and Lillian undressed her daughter like she did when Diana was a child. Diana didn't want to bother protesting this. Lillian started the shower, and Diana stepped in, while still wearing her underwear — unaware that she wasn't naked. Lillian climbed in behind her daughter, wrapped her arms around her and held her silently while the water fell on them.

"Thank you, mom."

"Of course."

"I know I'm a mess. Thank you for holding me."

"I always want you near."

After the women dried themselves and dressed, they went back downstairs to talk to Officer Jenkins. He was now standing in the foyer.

He had been waiting at the door. "I've got your statement. If I need anything more, I'll be in touch. Take care of yourself."

Diana settled into a chair at the kitchen table while her mother made tea. Just then, her father got home.

"Hold On, Hold On"
Neko Case

The door flung open.

"What the hell?! What the hell happened, Diana?! Did the police charge you yet?" The door was still open as he screamed into the house.

Diana had dreaded his arrival. She learned to dislike him most in doorways. It began when she was a little girl, and her father would enter her room at night to touch her, and to make her do the same to him. Though she didn't understand the acts then, she still detested them. He would pause and linger in the doorway on his way into her room. He was usually smelling of alcohol, and that helped her forgive him.

He saw Diana at the table and approached her.

"You're only eighteen, just old enough to be charged as an adult for running over that boy. I'm going to have to talk to that boy's father." The two women fell silent. They were uncomfortable with what they were hearing and at a loss as to what to do next. "His name was Sean," was all that Diana could muster.

The issues that were confronting him had been racing through his head, and he let them spill out into the kitchen. "They're gonna figure out that I own three dealerships and live in a big house. This is gonna cost me. That poor bugger lost his son, and this is also gonna cost me something."

Both women remained silent and averted their eyes. There was too much that bothered them about what he was saying to engage in a conversation.

"You okay?" he finally asked Diana. She nodded.

"Okay. Well, I'm going to figure out what's next. Maybe talk to the police and the boy's family."

"Sean."

"What?"

"His name is Sean."

"Fine."

Diana left the kitchen, headed up the stairs, entered her bedroom, crossed it and climbed out the window. She sat on the roof. It was as close to free as she could feel while being at her parents' house. Her father's concerns faded. *I have to let them fall away. My only concern is for Sean's family... I wish I could do something for them. I can't talk to dad. Mom won't do anything. She never does.*

The stars were coming out, one by one, she always loved watching them. Stars were such a common miracle. She had always loved the night sky, and at the age of sixteen, had borrowed a book from the library about constellations. She could identify a few. But this time, it was different. She didn't want to experience the joy of it. Her soul was convulsing again, as it did at the accident. Then it happened.

Everything around her seemed to be moving — the roof beneath her, the earth thirty feet below her. The colours blurred, and she felt her body sway. She looked up to the sky and searched for Orion. *Maybe it will anchor me,* she thought. It was always the most easily visible constellation in the night sky. The stars left their standard positions. They were moving, it seemed. She opened and closed her eyes, then shook her head. The lights in the sky were forming letters. Galaxies apart, the suns spelled four letters: F-L-E-E. And they burned brighter than usual. So powerful, it illuminated her face, the roof, her yard and the fields.

She stood and screamed to the night, drawing out the word, "NOOOOOOOO!"

When her mother appeared at her window, Diana quickly turned to her and then back to the sky. The message was gone. She couldn't hear her mother's words. She was reeling. She pushed past Lillian at her window, looked to her and said, "In the end, I'm just some mean girl." And then passed out on the floor of her bedroom.

"There Is An End"
The Greenhornes

Diana didn't attend the funeral. But she intended to do so. In the days after the accident, she caught snippets of conversation between her parents that concerned her. Words were hushed, and then she would hear her father's outbursts. She heard enough nouns and verbs from his explosion to form a sense of the issues. "Prison', "money", "pay-off", and "manslaughter" seemed to be the cause of the eruptions.

It's like I'm a ghost now. No one talks to me. I'm not to go out. I'm only spoken of – not to. The only way I know I'm alive is that they talk about my care and feeding. Am I hungry? No. Am I tired? Always. But I can't sleep. But I don't want to tell them. I don't want to talk to them, and they really don't want to talk to me. Just the thought of a conversation annoys me...

The day after the accident, her parents cornered her in the kitchen. She had come down to get tea.

Oh, god, what is this? It's like they were waiting for me to emerge so they could pounce on me. Why are they just standing there? I have nothing to say. I don't mind the awkward silence. It beats the alternative.

"Your mom and I were thinking that we should pay for the funeral. The event, gravestone and plot. The whole thing."

Quit searching me. What do you want from me? Yes, it's the least we could do, but I don't think we share a motivation. I'm just making tea. Keep making tea.

The long pause was ended by another announcement from Steve.

"Speaking of that. I'll be going to the funeral, but I think you should stay here." He seemed unsure. He was faltering. "Your mother and I think it would be for the best."

Diana quickly looked at him. *What's your game? He's trying to be strong. If I wait and stare at him, he will break. That means screaming. He's like those cheap tables with a glued top that couldn't stand up to a little bit of wear or water. Your veneer is peeling, Stevie.* This accident had deeply upset him. She could see it. The boy's death was obviously nothing less than a tragedy, but she could see his eyes were appealing to her for understanding. "Please, let me protect you," they seemed to be saying to her. She was caught between wanting to revolt and pitying this awkward act of love. So, she went to her default position with her father: forgiveness. She would just forgive him for trying to control the situation, and for trying to control her again.

But I have to make a decision. I've been dreading the funeral. What do I bring that poor boy's family except for anger? Nothing good comes from me being there. But I should be there. I want to do something for them. For him. But there's nothing.

She whispered, "I'll stay here."

"It'll be fine," he said. She could sense the relief in his voice.

Diana began to bristle. Fine? There was nothing fine about this. And maybe it was okay for him. There was no sense of sadness from him, no recognition of this tragedy. He was just happy that his daughter had escaped with no charges. And maybe he was happy about what that meant for him. He didn't understand that this would be something else she would have to carry. It marked her now. It was burned into her like a branding. This was who she was now — the girl from the accident where the boy died. The one who drove the car. You know, the girl that killed the kid.

"Nothing's fine."

"Right. Of course. Okay, I'm going to head out now. Take care of the arrangements."

Without another word, she made her way to the stairs to go back to her bedroom. He followed behind her but turned in the foyer to go out the front door. She felt tired and wanted to crawl beneath her blankets. She lay under the covers, staring at the ceiling, playing over all the details in her head. The birds outside were singing and chirping, and it only annoyed her. So, she pulled the blanket over her head. In the darkness, the accident played out again. She wept, and her mind turned to the other boy there. He was so young. They were both so young. With her index finger, she spelled out the letters F-L-E-E on the blankets.

She began to weep again until she heard someone gently knocking on the door. Diana ignored it. Lillian tried once more and then called to her daughter as she opened the door slightly. "Diana. I need to speak to you." Diana could feel the weight of her mother on the bed and emerged from beneath the blanket.

"I need you to listen to me for a moment."

Diana sat up straight in her bed. Her mother seemed forceful. She sat erect on the edge of the mattress.

"This is a terrible thing that happened, and I can only imagine how you must feel. Your father and I have cleared a path for you out of here and out of this mess, and you need to take it. We need to put this tragedy and this place behind you."

She paused, took a deep breath and added: "We also need to put this house behind you." With the last line, she looked directly into her daughter's eyes and nodded to her. Diana was stunned.

Her mother continued: "You need to go off to university this fall. For the summer, you need to go away from here. I spoke to my cousin, Marie, out west. She has a job for you. They have a ranch, and they're working the rodeo circuit, and you can go with them. You can work the horses."

Diana leaned forward, wrapped her arms around her mother, dropped her head onto her mom's shoulders and chest, and whispered a quiet "Thank you." She then began to cry. As she did, her mother stiffened. "There's no need for that, and we don't have time for it anyway. We need to get you packed up while your father is gone to arrange the funeral and his ridiculous staff barbecue."

While she showered, her mother packed her bags. In less than thirty minutes, Diana was in the car with her mother on the way to the train station in Belleville.

Diana stepped out of the car. Lilian didn't.

"Your bag's in the trunk. I'll pop it."

Diana gathered her belongings and waited for her mother. She walked to the front of the car and peered into the open window. Her mother looked away for a moment then turned to Diana.

"You need to get your ticket. You've got to get used to doing things on your own now," she added. Diana paused, and as she did, her mother reached out and grabbed her hand through the car window, kissing the back of it and placing it against the side of her own face. Diana could feel the tears. She bent down and kissed her mother on her forehead.

"I love you, mom. Thank you."

"I know, I know. I love you too."

"Bye, mom."

"Have your aunt call me when you get to the ranch."

Diana nodded.

In just over two hours, she was sitting on the train, heading west, and staring into the open space of Lake Ontario. It was the closest she felt to ease in the last three days. The train was moving fast. Unless she looked further away, everything was moving too quickly to discern the details. It made her head swim. She turned to the sky for answers, but it remained silent and grey.

There's an end to everything, and I guess it can look like this.

"Piano Concerto No. 4 in G Major, 2nd Movement"
Ludwig Van Beethoven

Diana would spend the next three days on trains.

Her mother had slipped five hundred dollars in the pocket of her jeans. She used some of the money to buy two books at the train station. One was called *Who Do You Think You Are*, and the other was a new book by her favourite childhood author, Madeleine L'Engle. She finished both of them before leaving the endless forests and lakes of Ontario.

Why didn't I buy more books? I don't want to think about my own life.

She tried to talk to other travellers but had a hard time avoiding their prying questions. She had a sleeper car but rarely slept in it. She retreated to it repeatedly to avoid conversations and watch the landscape passing her window. After the first night, which had been riddled with terrible dreams of the accident, she fought sleep. At night she would peer out past the window as the Canadian wilderness swept by, searching upward for direction. Nothing came.

The days began to pass quickly, and she grew anxious as she pulled into the train station in Edmonton.

No one knows me. What's my problem? Except for Marie. She will know me. Of course she knows what happened.

She recognized her aunt Marie even though it had been three summers since she had visited. She had her mother's dark hair but a more open, easy way about her. Tall in her jeans, t-shirt, and cowboy boots, she was every part the rancher. Just as much as her husband, Tom. They had met in college in Ontario and shared a love of horses and the outdoors, especially the Rocky Mountains. Tom was from Alberta and had grown up on the ranch. As the eldest son, his father passed it on to him. It was a sprawling affair on the foothills of the Rockies, a few hundred kilometers southwest of Edmonton.

"Well, Diana, haven't you grown into a beautiful thing," said her aunt. Diana felt her aunt was searching her face. *Yeah, she knows.* Diana didn't want to talk about it with her aunt.

"Hi, Aunt Marie. Thanks for coming to get me."

"It's no trouble, my dear. We're glad to have you, and we could use the help this summer. Your uncle Tom and your cousin, Brett, are already on the road. I've got hands helping me at the ranch, but I've also got to deal with tourists. All the oil chasers come out for a weekend getaway. They pay a high price, so we have a few cabins."

Tom had been a champion calf roper in rodeos across the west, down into the States. His son, Brett, now nineteen, was competing on the circuit under his father's tutelage. It usually took them away for a lot of the summer.

Her aunt picked her up from the train station in a worn and dusty Chevy K-Series pickup truck. The idea of getting into a vehicle gave her pause, but she got in, and her aunt started along the roads out of the city and back to the ranch. Diana sat on her hands, gripping the seat at times.

"It's gonna take a couple of hours to get out to the ranch. I thought I'd let you have a day or two to rest on the ranch, and then you could catch up with them on the road. Tom may come back home and let you stay on the road with Brett if all goes well. Sound all right to you?"

Diana could sense the concern in her aunt's voice. She didn't want pity, but now that she was with her and having to have the longest conversation she had in three days, she wanted another portion of silence. The best way to achieve that was to appear fine and speak about another subject.

Diana nodded. "I'm looking forward to seeing your ranch. I love horses."

"Well, that's good."

Diana continued to talk about horses and the work she had done with them until they arrived just before 4:00 p.m. Diana had never been to the ranch before. But she loved the long driveway and the rolling hills. Her aunt slowed the truck as they drove down the gravel lane.

"Those are our wild roses you see there," said Marie.

The flowers were growing all along the driveway. She turned to the open window of the truck and felt the warm wind and sun on her face. She closed her eyes and released her hands from beneath her thighs. The air was filled with perfume. There was a lot of space and so few people. She sighed and felt at ease for a few moments.

The weeks passed quickly for Diana. With new work, new people, and new experiences, she found herself distracted and happy for the diversions. She was travelling around western Canada and the United States with her cousin. She helped to take care of the horses and kept on top of the paperwork for each rodeo. She didn't want to drive. She left that to Brett. He had asked her once, on their first day of driving, if she could take over for him.

"It's been a long haul. You wanna take over after we get gas?"

Diana was startled. She shifted in her seat. No, she didn't want to drive. She wanted to yell this at him but, instead, looked out the window, and uttered a strained, "No."

Brett went silent, glanced at her, and then realized the issue. He never asked again.

It was only at night before sleep when she was alone that she found herself breathless. Anxiety would rear up in her. Her mind would turn to the accident when she closed her eyes to sleep. It would come in sudden, intense flashes: the sound and feel of hitting Sean, his small bloody body, his face. She would push the images out of her head by opening her eyes. When she did fall asleep, the images would often re-appear in dreams. Generally, she woke up nearly as tired as when she went to sleep.

"It's My Way"
Buffy Sainte-Marie

It was August, and they had travelled to eastern Alberta for the Bonnyville Rodeo. Marie had organized to sell a horse that Brett and Diana brought with them, and they had to deliver to Fort McMurray after the event. It would take some five hours to get there and then another ten or so back to the ranch. They had a few days to get it done.

They stopped at a little diner just outside Fort McMurray. They had planned to stay, have dinner and then bring the horse to its new owner. They pulled into the parking lot beside the small restaurant on the edge of the town and noticed a man standing near the entrance to the lot with some sort of papers in his hand. He approached their truck. He was tall, in his forties, with short, dark hair and a dark complexion. Diana quickly realized he was indigenous. She knew this part of the province had a sizable Cree population.

"Can I give you some information?" The man asked in a calm and quiet tone.

She didn't trust her cousin's response, so she jumped in. "Yeah, sure. What's going on?"

"Well, they're going to start pulling oil from the sands north of here. The process will involve a lot of pollution that's going to run into the Athabasca River. It's not going to be good for us."

"Then why are they doing it?" she asked.

"Well, money, I guess. With all of the noise about oil overseas, everyone is looking for new places to get it."

"Well, does the government know about this?"

"Yeah, they'll likely make a lot of money too. Them, and the oil company. Not me, or my community. We will just have to deal with our waters becoming polluted and the land disturbed."

Diana was incensed. "What can we do?"

"Well, take this information I have about it. After you read it, you can sign my petition if you're still interested."

"Okay, I will."

Diana was preoccupied during lunch. She kept watching this man in the parking lot. The few people who had stopped here seemed to be locals. They knew him, ignored him, and he responded in-kind. She read through the materials while her cousin chewed his French fries.

Brett glanced at what she was reading. "They've always got a problem. First, it's treaties, and now it's this."

Diana remained silent. Living where she did in Ontario, she had little experience with indigenous people. Tyendinaga, Mohawk Territory, was south of her on the lake. But there was an invisible wall between the territory and the nearby community. As Brett continued eating, she ignored her lunch, got up from the table without a word and walked back outside. Brett had noticed that she seemed bothered all summer. She often took time for herself. So, he didn't say anything as she left.

The man was still standing in the parking lot when she got out there.

"I'd like to sign your petition."

He smiled. "One sec, it's in my truck."

He walked over to the edge of the parking lot to his truck, emerged with some papers on a clipboard, and returned to her.

"Here you go. And thanks."

"No problem. What else can I do?"

"Well, we're having a protest at the site tomorrow. You can come. The more people, the better." He smiled, "Especially people who look like you."

"I'll be there," she replied. She offered no smile in return, but felt resolute. It was the first time this summer she was sure of something.

"Okay. We'll be starting around 8:00 a.m. when the day shift starts. Just head north, and you'll see the signs for CrudeCor."

She walked back to the diner. Brett looked up as she approached the table.

"So, you signed it, huh?"

"Yeah. And tomorrow morning, you're on your own. I'm going to protest with them. We can leave after it's done."

"Jesus Christ," he muttered and looked around the room for the waitress to get the cheque.

"We have plenty of time to get back to the ranch."

When they arrived at the hotel, after dropping off the horse, she had asked him for the car keys to get something she said she had left in the vehicle. She took them to her room. She didn't want to talk further about her plans, and now she could just do it. But, as soon as the metal of the keys touched her hand, she grew anxious.

If I'm going to do this, I have to drive myself.

Diana had a fitful sleep. The old nightmare returned. She woke up, nauseous, at 5:00 a.m. She quickly scrawled a note for Brett. "See you at lunch. D"

Why do I feel rushed? She stepped out of her motel room and felt a rush of cool night air. Sunrise was an hour away. *I want to see what I'm protesting. I want to be prepared.* She slipped the note under Brett's door. She was sweating as she got into the driver's seat of the truck. The nausea grew. Her eyes stung from the lack of sleep.

Was the engine always this loud? Right. This isn't so bad. I remember this. Thank god there aren't any other cars out here.

She followed the highway to Fort McMurray and Lake Mildred, just as she had been told the day before. There were few cars, and the sky was turning from the deep, inky black to a shade of blue that always gave her comfort. It was rich and hopeful with the promise of a new day.

She saw the signs for CrudeCor. Bright and hopeful signs. As though it was a theme park. She arrived at the oil sands project site and felt she had entered a city from the future. Some metropolis devoid of people and nature where only the machinery lived. It was as though someone pushed her backwards. The site was such an affront. There were buildings and smokestacks, pavement, and pipes. It was still early in the day, so there were few people there. Everything was paved.

The air smelled strange—like fresh pavement mixed with ammonia and rotten eggs. It was a terrible combination.

She was sitting in the truck at the site entrance when a car drove up to the gates and startled her. She immediately started the engine, moved to the right, and then circled the parking lot before leaving. She drove down the highway until she found a sideroad. She pulled onto the gravel road, parked the truck, and stepped out.

She felt a sense of purpose and clarity that she hadn't felt in months. Her mind turned to her cousin and the conversations they had last night. They had developed a friendly relationship—like siblings—but his apparent disregard for the already struggling people troubled her. It was systemic racism. As though the Cree, Chipewyan and Metis had no right to have concerns. Or, even worse, they just didn't matter. From the materials given to her by the man in the parking lot, she learned that some of these concerns were based on treaties centuries-old that had not been honoured by the provincial and federal government. She became incensed all over again. It also struck her that their concerns about pollution were also vital to non-indigenous residents in the area.

The fire was growing in her. She had felt splintered, tired and old for eighteen, but this made her feel whole, purposeful and filled with energy. The stars were beginning to disappear. She watched them. *I can always count on you, Orion.*

She watched in surprise as the mythic figure put down his bow, signalled for the dog, Canis Major, to come to him, and formed the stars across the night sky into something new. The letters spelled a single word: F-I-G-H-T. Just like before, they shone brighter and lit the gravel, hills, and air around her. She felt a warmth on her face and tears streamed down her cheeks.

"Okay," she whispered in return. The stars pulsed and faded into the sky. She watched the sun make its ascent in the east. The mallards floating on Athabasca River began their lonesome song with the arrival of sunlight. She could feel the motion of the world around her waking. Joy crept into her that turned to love for the world around her.

I've got a way I'm going now and it's my own path.

As the sun appeared fully above the horizon, she turned to it. "And what do you have to say for yourself?" She was surprised to hear herself laugh in the quiet of the morning in the wilderness.

The protesters were to meet at the entrance of the plant. When she arrived, there was a small group there. She recognized the man from the parking lot the other day. He saw her, too, and waved her over.

"Hey, Tony, Don, this is Diana," he said, introducing her to the two men standing near him. She said nothing and shook their hands. Of the twenty-or-so people there, she noticed she was one of the few that were white.

"I didn't get your name the other day," Diana said.

"George," he replied. "We've got some placards in the back of Donna's truck," he continued. "You want to grab one?"

She walked toward the truck and saw a series of signs. The one she chose, read: "OIL AND WATER DON'T MIX!"

The protesters planned to start at 8:30 a.m. when the gates would open and the workers would arrive. She joined the others with the placards. Cars began to move towards the plant, and they had to slow down to enter the gates. That's where Diana and the other protestors stood chanting. "Quit poisoning us! Quit poisoning us!"

Most of the workers rolled up their windows and looked the other way. One man kept his window open, and as he drove by, screamed: "Get back to the reservation." He then threw a half-empty beer can that barely missed one of the protesters, but sent beer across Diana's shirt and onto several protester's shoes. The tossed can sent a wave of silence through the crowd.

The man's car sped and screeched across the pavement. Diana was livid. The truck was just about to pass her. She moved towards the speeding vehicle and kicked it twice — on the driver's door and just behind the rear wheel.

"Pig!" She screamed. He countered with "Bitch!"

He continued past her, and she continued to follow his truck. The other protesters quickly grew concerned and stepped in between Diana and the vehicle. George placed his hand on her shoulder and spoke quietly, but urgently "Diana, it's okay." She instinctively threw his arm back and wheeled around to face him. He looked shocked and stepped back.

She was surprised by her own response. She stopped and nodded to him but didn't say a word. In the moments that followed, others began to sing her praises. Security guards appeared on the other side of the gate and stood ominously, staring down the group and talking on radios. They didn't speak directly to the protestors. After about an hour of traffic with no incidents, it came to an end.

George approached her. "You're a natural at this. Thank you for your support."

"Thank you... Thanks for letting me be here," she said, feeling both shy and mighty.

"Isobel"
Björk

As August ended, Diana was preoccupied with what the autumn held for her. The person she was a few months ago, who had planned to go to the University of Guelph with interest in becoming a veterinarian, seemed distant to her. It was only a few short days before she would go, and the thought of sitting in a classroom made her feel anxious, restless.

As she rode the train to Toronto, she had time to think about what was coming next. She knew something was going to change. A demand from within herself was emerging. A request that would not be denied.

Her mother met her at Union Station in Toronto. Lillian had filled their truck with Diana's belongings. Diana was relieved when she found out that her father wouldn't be there. But when she arrived at Union Station, she felt guilty because the sight of her mother didn't bring her happiness. It was like two polarities with the same charge meeting. The closer her mother got to her, the more Diana wanted to push her away.

"You look thin," Lillian said as she embraced her daughter in the busy hall of the train station.

Diana looked over her mother's shoulder at the current of other passengers moving through the massive train station. She stepped back.

"Yeah, I guess."

Lillian picked up one of her daughter's bags and continued speaking. "You're going to love Guelph."

Diana wanted to share her mother's excitement and tried her best to do so. As they entered the parking garage, Lillian continued talking.

"You'll probably meet some new girlfriends, and you can get a place in Guelph after your first year."

"Yeah, maybe."

"Well, I'll help get you settled in today, and then I'll head back home."

"Okay."

Diana stopped in her tracks. She saw the truck. Her mother had needed their largest vehicle to bring all of her belongings. Steve had put the cab on it to protect her belongings. But it was still the vehicle from the accident.

"You know your father wishes he was here, but he just couldn't get away."

Diana remained silent. Her heart rate increased, and she had a hard time breathing. But she didn't want to share this with her mother. She consciously pushed herself forward towards the truck and remained silent. Diana opened the passenger door, stepped in, and immediately rolled down the window. She pushed her face through the open window for air. Her mother hopped in the driver seat of the vehicle.

"The city just gets busier and busier. I don't mind telling you that I don't love driving up here."

The day continued like this, with Lillian being the purveyor of excitement and Diana the reluctant participant. Diana was relieved when her mother drove away in the truck. She then felt terrible for it. For the last two months, she had been on the move. She liked that. She also liked the feeling of purpose and clarity she had at the protest. That first night she walked around the campus thinking of these things. It was then that the idea of being a veterinarian fell away from her. And in its place, environmental science emerged.

Being a protector of vulnerable lands. That's something that I can do. I will forge a deal with nature.

That week, she changed her courses and joined the environmental club. While other students enjoyed their frosh week beer kegs, marijuana, and parties, she was in lineups to change her major. She joined the environmental club and met with a few members. When she spoke of her experiences at the protest, she gained admiration from the members and could sense it. She enjoyed it. So, she began to talk to them about the most pressing environmental issues in the area.

The club was her main focus at the university. She loved studying environmental science but the culture of classrooms and sitting around talking left her feeling bothered and bored. She needed action. So, university life became a series of assignments and essays that she would finish between events, organizing, letter writing and meetings. Her methods were brilliant and fearless, and her passion palpable. One of her professors told her, "You raise wonderful hell."

She led all central Ontario protests, and that became province-wide. But any project that would take her to her hometown and the surrounding area were handled by a colleague. Diana made sure of that. She also worked through the holidays to have excuses not to return for any reason.

As the anniversary of the accident arrived, her mother called her more frequently. Diana was surprised by the increase in the number of calls. Until finally, on the day of the accident, after trying several times to reach Diana, Lillian just asked her.

"Are you okay?"

"I'm fine. Why do you keep asking me that?"

There was a pause. She could hear her mother sigh.

"It's been a year, you know... since the accident."

A silence fell. *Oh my god, I forgot. I can't tell her that. What's wrong with me?*

"Thanks, mom. I'm okay. It's nice of you to call and ask me."

"Well, okay. I just wanted to make sure."

After the call ended, Diana realized it was the first time she'd spoken about it for almost a year.

"No Agreement"
Fela Kuti

Diana had energy, a shared purpose and the dark thoughts faded. Sleep was a short burst, but she appreciated it. She knew that if she slept longer, there was a good chance the nightmares would start again. That seemed worse than being a little tired.

After her first year of university, she was hired by an environmental group to lead a series of protests off the west coast of Canada. She continued with the organization when she was back at school, leading campaigns in Toronto and across Ontario. This was a pattern that continued for Diana. She studied at the university and worked for various similar organizations during the summer break and through the school year.

After she graduated, she moved into a full-time job with The Environmental Justice Network, leading campaigns in Canada and the United States. She was busy, generally celebrated by her peers, maligned by some in the business community and in politics. Diana's methods also alienated her from a portion of her colleagues.

She'd been arrested for mischief, trespassing, public disturbances, and assault. She was impatient with the rate of change in environmental and social justice. The more she worked, the more extreme her methods grew. She could feel her life gaining speed. In her mind, the equation was simple. She was serving a purpose and would use whatever means were needed to be of service. It wasn't complicated. If others couldn't understand that, it wasn't her problem. Her mind would often go back to the message from Orion that early morning in Alberta.

That's the day my life began again. I need to trust that. That's all there is now.

Many of her friends and colleagues had been arrested for minor infractions like trespassing and disturbing the peace. They were typically jailed and then released. It was a standard method to stop protests. Diana was becoming famous for going a step further. She had broken into facilities to get samples, records, take pictures or leave graffiti. When she was met with opposition at protests, Diana became increasingly antagonistic towards her opponents, baiting them to violence.

She was threatened at a protest in Sioux Falls, and the man who had uttered the threat received a punch in the face from Diana. As she entered her thirties, an increasingly loud chorus both within the organization and movement were critical of Diana. Her arrests had led to convictions, she had been placed on probation, and received restraining orders. It was getting hard for her to get approval to lead campaigns. The final act that led to a career shift occurred in the Puget Sound.

Diana had joined with EcoWarriors to fight the whalers in the Pacific. After months of successful interventions with Japanese whaling boats, the protestors' ship made it back to the Pacific coast and was moored in Puget Sound near Seattle. Her shipmates were unaware that the Coast Guard and local police had been advised by the FBI to board the ship, interrogate the crew, and formally charge the leadership for shipping infractions.

Diana had been on the deck of the ship at dawn, sipping coffee and enjoying the sunrise when they arrived. A member of the crew, Marty, heard their voices on the megaphone, demanding they lower a ladder to allow the four officers to access the ship. Diana heard the commotion and began to walk to the stern of the ship. She arrived to see Marty in cuffs, being pushed against the railing along the ship's edge.

"What the hell?" was all she could offer.

"Raise your hands," a member of the Coast Guard yelled.

Diana complied.

Guns? Really. You're nervous. Why are you afraid of us? I guess that's why you have your guns out...

"What the hell are you doing?"

"Drinking coffee. You?"

"Don't get smart. Get your ass beside your comrade!"

As he shouted this order, he advanced towards Diana. The deck was slippery from an overnight rain, and as he fumbled for a set of handcuffs on his belt, he slid on the deck. Diana instinctively reached out to help him. Marty was too far away to be of assistance.

"Get your hands in the air!" he shouted in response.

She had just reached his shoulder when he shouted. She withdrew, and he continued to fall forward.

"I guess you're swimming then," she responded flatly as his body flew past her and against the railing.

A silence fell on everyone on deck, followed by a scream and a splash.

"Idiots," she muttered, looking over the railing.

Diana was arrested. News reports stated that protestors had pushed a member of the coast guard over the side of their ship. The man had been rescued, but Diana was charged with assaulting an officer. Marty came to her defence, along with one of the police officers. There was no agreement on the details of the accident. The charges were dismissed. But damage was done to her reputation. So, she finally took an office job with The Environmental Justice Network. Her new role was in developing strategies and campaigns for others to enact. She was ready to accept it.

I need to take my foot off the gas. At least for a little while.

That was when she met Mark. He was a field biologist and was often brought in as an expert by The Environmental Justice Network. He was a couple of years older than her, tall, slim, and calm. At first, she thought maybe he was dull. When he spoke, he did so with a quiet, determined authority without a hint of aggression. His tone was matter-of-fact. She appreciated it. She wanted to explore, but felt tentative.

Mark was smitten with her. He'd heard of her before he met her and was surprised at how easy she was to get along with, contrary to his preconceived notions. Her reputation as a militant activist led him to believe that she would be blustery, angry, and demanding. But in fact, he enjoyed talking to her and found her energetic and engaging—if maybe a little distracted.

She initiated the relationship. Mark made no demands of her. He was often away, and he loved living outdoors. He kept an apartment in Toronto, but soon they moved in together. She felt he was like a sweater in the fall. One of those she owned for years, could put away and then rely upon later for warmth and comfort. Mark knew that there was a distance between them, and perhaps in time, he would travel it. But for now, he was happy to have time with her in the city when he wasn't in the field.

There was an unspoken agreement between them to not push the relationship further. He felt her desire for it, and his passion for her made it bearable. He knew this was the price of being with Diana.

So, life continued like this for Diana for a few years, through the mid-nineties into the new millennium's early years. There was a repose, ease in her life. She attempted to settle into it with Mark. There was a slow rhythm to her life of work in Toronto with travel and guest lectures.

Mark would come and go. She was growing to accept it. She found the nights and her weekends the most difficult. Until now, Diana rarely had free time in her life, and now that she did have it, she didn't enjoy it. So, she began to work later and on weekends. In her free time, she would convince her colleagues to go out for drinks. They loved hearing her stories from protests. She grew to like drinking red wine. Later, she relied on it to maintain peace in this
static existence.

"Sinnerman"
Nina Simone

Diana's life moved at this new pace until the day one of her colleagues, an activist named Victoria Munera, disappeared. Victoria was about ten years younger than Diana. She was one of the people Diana hired, trained, and sent into the field. Originally from Colombia, Victoria expressed an urge to return to her home country. There were labour issues growing over the last ten years in Bogotá. Recently, union organizers from a soda bottling company owned by an American firm were threatened, disappeared, and were found murdered by paramilitary groups. Victoria wanted to respond. It was outside of the scope of The Environmental Justice Network, so Diana connected Victoria with the local chapter of the Federal Union of Public Employees. They hired Victoria to join in an international response by unions. Victoria had strict rules to report weekly. She missed one deadline. Diana tried to reach her at the phone number she'd been given in Colombia. After two days of calling, she finally got someone.

"No, no. Victoria, not here. Victoria is gone," was all she got from the woman's voice on the other end of the phone.

"Where is she?"

"Victoria is gone."

"Where did she go?"

"No one know." The woman hung up.

Diana stood in her office, holding the phone. This was her fear. Diana had given her strict instructions to meet, gather information, and report back—and together, they would come up with a plan. It had been two months since Victoria had arrived in Colombia. She sensed Victoria wanted to do more. Diana was trying to slow her down. She knew this wasn't her strongest skill, but she tried. And now, Victoria was missing. She slammed down the phone and marched into the office of Liam Bishop, the president of The Environmental Justice Network.

"Liam, I need to go to Colombia right away," she announced.

Liam looked up from his computer. "What?"

"Victoria is missing. She missed a reporting deadline, as you know. I've been trying to get hold of her, and all I know is that she's gone. That's all they can tell me. And you know Victoria wouldn't just take off."

Liam pushed back from his desk and sighed. "I'm so sorry. But we need to start with the official channels. Let's call the embassy and get them to work with the local authorities."

"Are you kidding me? They don't care at all. If something happened to her, they're likely responsible for it!"

"But they need to know we're following up on it, that we're watching them. And I'll reach out to the union and all the other agencies and NGOs operating there, and we will find her. She's probably fine. Maybe she just couldn't make it to a computer or the internet is out or something."

"That's not enough. We're responsible for her. She's just a kid."

"Then what do you want me to do?"

"I want you to put me on a plane to Bogotá."

"Diana, what are you gonna do there?"

"I'm going to find her. And I'm going to bring her home."

I'm tired of this. I'm not explaining myself. Diana started to walk out of his office.

Liam continued, even though he knew she couldn't hear him. "Diana, c'mon... where are you gonna run to?"

She passed on the elevator for the stairs, walked out the front door, and hailed a cab.

"I need you to take me to Pearson."

"The airport?"

"Yeah, the airport. Sorry. One stop. I just need to grab my passport, and then I can go."

"Okay."

"And please hurry."

"A Dios le Pido"
Juanes

It was three weeks since Diana arrived in Colombia. She was now sleeping in Victoria's apartment in the town of Carepa in northern Colombia.

She had contracted a virus and had been laid up in bed for two days. She was alone, her stomach churned, and she had not found Victoria.

When she arrived in Bogotá and spoke to her contacts at the union, they told her that Victoria had been conducting interviews with witnesses in northern Colombia, near the border with Panama. Four union organizers had been killed, including the union president. He had been executed on factory lands. The remaining workers were reportedly held at gunpoint by a small, armed group and forced to resign from the union. Immediately after this incident, the Unión Alimentaria left the region. Victoria had told the union leaders in Bogotá that she would go to Carepa to confirm these stories.

There was now no union presence in the area, and they had few contacts in Carepa. So, Diana had no one to call. Instead, she convinced the organization to provide a driver who could also act as an interpreter and drove her to the city. If she had flown, they were afraid it would draw suspicion. Few people flew to Carepa, and the paramilitaries and the government monitored the flights.

The driver, Gustavo, was a wiry man in his thirties with thick, dark hair. He was energetic, and this trip had him nervous. So, his energy was an electrical arc, buzzing and sharp. But he was kind. He understood the gravity of the situation and was committed to helping Diana. He sensed a great force in Diana and worried about her. But she typically brushed aside his concerns.

When they started the journey, he told her, "I am here to not just interpret the language and drive, but to keep you

AIN'T NOTHIN' BUT A STRANGER IN THIS WORLD

safe. I will be your friend whether you like it or not. And all my friends call me Gus. So, you call me Gus."

"I appreciate it, Gus. I'm honoured to call you my friend, but I don't need anyone keeping me safe."

It was a two-day drive. The country was beautiful. The people she met at the gas stations and tiny restaurants were kind and spoke in passionate tones. She drove through the day, studying the plants, the faces and reading the signs for towns, cities and other destinations. She needed to do something on the long drive to distract her mind. She hadn't packed clothes, let alone a book. So, she practiced the names of places. They were ornate and energetic in her mouth: Medellin, Barranquilla, Macando...

She planned to meet two factory employees in their home. The night was the safest time to do this. She had to park a few blocks away and walk with Gus. Now that Diana had been forced to slow down to consider the risk Gus was taking, she felt bad about having him with her. She wanted to let him stay in the car, but her Spanish was weak. So, she walked in front of him. If there was trouble coming for them, she wanted to face it.

When they arrived at the house, she looked around to make sure no one was watching them. She read the note from the union staff: "73 Carrera, three houses north of Calle 82, on the right side. A red house. Don't ask for a name. Don't give your name."

The street was rough, packed dirt with small trees and shrubs growing on it indiscriminately. She could hear murmurs of conversations and radios. She could smell food cooking. But she could see no one. When she arrived at the entrance, she noticed her hand shook as she raised it to knock on the door. Gus stepped forward and grabbed her arm. His hand was sweaty. He made a low hissing and clicking noise.

Then he made it again. The door opened. It was dark, and Diana saw the outlines of two people. They stood just inside the door. Gus stepped forward and whispered, "Victoria Munera?" The men whispered back to him, and she could only hear "de pronto" and "fotografia." She knew the second word meant photograph. She reached into her backpack and pulled out a picture of Victoria that the union members had provided to her. The men spoke in even quieter tones so she couldn't hear them, but she saw them nodding. Gus began to back away and took her by the wrist. She removed her arm from his grasp but followed him out. The door closed on their heels.

Diana began. "So, do they know?"

"No, not here," Gus whispered.

They hurried back to the car in silence. As he started the car, he turned to her. He looked in her eyes tenderly, paused and said: "She's gone."

"Gone?"

"Si. Gone."

"She went somewhere else, or..."

"Yes. Or. She was taken by men. She will not come back. I'm sorry."

Diana fell into silence. Gus began to drive.

"Where do we go?" he asked.

"To her apartment."

"We can go tomorrow when it is light."

"No. I want to go now."

They had arranged to stay at a hotel in the business district, but Diana didn't want to go there now. Gus shook his head but continued driving, and in a few minutes, they reached the street of Victoria's apartment.

"Just drop me there, and I will find you tomorrow," said Diana as she prepared to get out of the car.

"It's not safe."

"I know. Thank you."

Gus shook his head.

When she arrived, she realized that she didn't think about how she would get into the building. But when she got there, she found that the door was unlocked. It was on the second floor, above a store, not far from downtown Carepa. It was a studio. She immediately recognized Victoria's bag in the corner of the room. She had it with her in the office the morning she left for Colombia. She sat on the bed in the room and wept. She lay awake most of the night, tossed between regret and the logistics that needed her attention. At sunrise, she went downstairs. Gus was waiting for her.

"Good morning," he offered.

She was touched to find him waiting for her. She sensed the empathy in his voice. She summoned all of the kindness she could muster to return the sentiment with a smile. "Good morning, Gus."

As she got into the car, she told him of her plans. "I need to make phone calls."

"It is best to do it from our hotel."

They drove to the hotel. Her stomach felt acidic. She quickly came to the realization that all there was left to do was to make difficult phone calls to her colleagues, friends, and the authorities. After a morning of this, she felt exhausted, angry, and impotent. Gus had stayed at her side, bringing coffee and water.

"I want to go back to her apartment."

"It's not a good idea. It's not safe. They may watch it."

"I don't care. They won't do anything to me. They expected me to come. And they know there is nothing I can do."

"Okay. But why, Diana?"

"I just need to."

Her stomach continued to feel terrible. She assumed it was stress and a lack of sleep. She had experienced this before. She lay in Victoria's bed all afternoon. She was tossed between great shame and regret as well as a close analysis of all the steps that had led Victoria here. What could she have done differently to save Victoria? What could she do now? Her stomach churned and felt as though it was grinding. She ran to the bathroom.

The next day continued like this. She would get up, go to the hotel with Gus, get her messages, and make phone calls. Then she would retreat back to Victoria's room. She was only eating chicken broth and drinking coffee—a fever set in.

By the third day, she didn't get out of bed. She had lost her colleague, likely to a violent death, and she was gravely ill. She writhed on the mattress, then vomited and rolled over, away from it, gasping for air.

Sobbing, she continued, "I didn't know, Victoria... I didn't know this would happen... Sean." *Who is Sean?*, she thought, bewildered. Memories formed. *Why Sean now?* She vomited on the blanket and sheets again. She could hear voices in Spanish out on the street and the sound of the traffic. The air was hot, stale, and humid. She began to weep.

She wrapped her arms around a pillow and felt something. What? She pulled it out. It was a bag of jelly beans. Perplexed, she tossed them to the floor.

Her thoughts circled around the name Sean again. And the accident began to replay in her mind. She was rushing. Then the horror and despair of the sight of the boy lying on the street with his friend holding him in his arms. "Oh my god," she whispered to herself and vomited on the bed again. She curled herself into a ball, sobbing.

Will I die of this? Maybe I should. I only wanted to be of service, didn't I? My god, I need a rest.

"Beneath the Southern Cross"
Patti Smith

Gus finally entered the apartment just after 8:00 a.m. the following day and found Diana writhing slowly on the mattress, surrounded by vomit.

"You need to go home," he told her gravely.

"I know," she answered quietly, wincing.

"Come on," he said and picked her up from the bed.

She was delirious with fever. He gathered her belongings and helped her down the stairs to his car. He laid her down in the back seat. She could not resist. They drove all day and through the night. She would yell for him to stop at times so she could go to the bathroom on the side of the road. He would also stop for gas and bottled water. At dawn, they arrived in Bogotá. She was barely conscious when she was carried into the hospital. She remembered lights and voices, followed by silence and then darkness.

She woke up and found herself in a hospital room with a solution running into her body. Her stomach was settled, but she was exhausted.

"Hello?" she muttered. And then louder: "Hello!"

A nurse arrived. "Si?"

"Donde," she tried to piece together the phrase.

"At the hospital," the nurse replied.

"Okay. Why?"

"Just one moment."

The nurse disappeared and returned with a doctor.

"Good morning!" said the doctor. He was tall, animated, and had a moustache that was so large and tailored that it was almost comical to her. If she could have summoned laughter, she would have.

"What happened?" she asked.

"Well, you had Yellow Fever. It was an extreme case that led to shock to your organs. Fortunately, you are a strong woman and will recover. Some do not."

This exchange exhausted her, and then she remembered Victoria. She began to weep, covering her face. But there were no tears. She was dehydrated.

I'm ridiculous. I can't even cry.

"There, there. Rest. You will be better soon enough and then you can go home. To Canada, correct?"

Diana didn't answer.

It was a week before she was strong enough to travel. Over that week, one train of thought persisted: *I want out of this hospital. But where do I go? I can't go back to Toronto. I just can't face them.*

On the day of her release, she hailed a cab outside the hospital and gave the driver the address for Victoria's apartment. She began to sweat as she reached Victoria's street. Even more so as she climbed the stairs.

It smells like bleach. Gus must have cleaned up.

She sat on the edge of the bed and stared into the room. Her last days in this place were so foggy. Her thoughts turned to her last few hours in the space. Nausea and despair set in. *Sean. I get it. Sean's death mirrored Victoria's. Both died too young. And, of course, both were my fault. I can't deny it. Responsibility, I'm responsible. There was nothing I could do for either of them. Useless.* She punched the bed.

She got up. Outside, she found an internet cafe and sent a two-line email to Liam at the office: "I'll be travelling for the foreseeable future. I will keep in touch."

Diana was avoiding people. She had told Mark not to come and see her. She had heard that a funeral was being arranged for Victoria by her family in Toronto. She couldn't bear attending it and didn't feel she had the right to be there.

I want no one near me. Not a single person speaking to me. All I desire is nothing. I've never wished for nothing so much.

She purchased a one-way plane ticket to Mexico City. She had never been to Mexico. Her only plan was to be in the city, then travel, and learn Spanish.

A new language. Every word will be unknown to me. Each person who utters a sound will be a stranger. I won't be anyone to them. This is as close to happiness as I can muster.

As she boarded the plane, she paused.

I never said goodbye to Gus.

"Someday"
Los Lobos

Mexico City was perfect. She could lose herself in it. No one knew her. No one cared to know her except the occasional man who harassed her. She quickly spurned them. She holed up in an apartment and took long walks through the streets to public squares, museums, galleries, cafes, and restaurants. Spanish classes were in the evening.

The nights troubled her. Diana would quickly walk home at night after her classes. She felt rushed, as though she was running to or from something. But it had no name. She didn't know the destination. One night, when she was walking through a park to her apartment, the stars caught her attention. They seemed to be shining so bright. And a voice within urged her to look away.

Don't look up there. God knows what they'll ask of you. You've done enough.

She wanted no demands. Not even from the voiceless sky.

After three months of this, she rented a car and took to the roads, travelling first to the Pacific coast. The ocean was a balm. She would spend days on the beach, reading, walking, and swimming. Diana sent an occasional missive to her mother, Mark, and a few colleagues and friends.

I need to keep up a level of communication to retain autonomy. Otherwise, they'll assemble a search party for me.

When asked about her plans, all she could muster was, "Some day, I will go home."

It was on the Pacific Coast that she began to spend time with a fellow traveller. Angela was from Italy and was often the only other person on the beach at dawn. Angela spoke little English, and Diana spoke no Italian, so they communicated in the Spanish they were both learning.

Diana loved Angela's presence. She was energetic and joyous. Her hips were broad, and her skin was olive and tanned. Diana had lost weight with her illness and still felt weak, but being near Angela made her feel less lithe and pale.

The two women would swim together, and as the days progressed and Diana followed Angela back to her room one morning for a shower, she found a new comfort.

"Te gustaría ducharte?"

Diana paused.

I knew this was coming. And I do want it. Yes, I do want to shower with you. I need it. It's been so long. I feel so awkward.

"Si."

After rinsing the salt from their bodies and washing it from each other's hair, Angela turned to her.

"Puedo lavarte el cabello?"

Diana paused. *It's so intimate. No one has washed my hair since I was a child.*

"Si, gracias."

Angela smiled and gently massaged shampoo into Diana's hair. She then rinsed it while protecting Diana's eyes from the soap running onto her face. As Angela reached for the conditioner, Diana pulled her close and kissed her firmly on the lips. After the kiss, they dried off and moved to the bed.

Diana lay on her back and felt like she was floating while Angela kissed and touched her body. After she orgasmed, she immediately fell into a deep sleep. When she awoke hours later, she was shocked at how good she felt.

The women continued like this for a week. Until Angela's questions about Diana became more persistent.

Here I go again. I do this to everyone. I give too little, and then I'm gone... It's just like high school with Francine. I left without even saying goodbye. And I never returned her calls. What do I tell them? All I can give you will only hurt you, and you'll be left with ashes.

She quit going to the beach in the morning. She had always ensured they went to Angela's room so she could choose when to leave, and she would never have to worry about Angela showing up at her door. Just as quickly as it started, it ended.

She decided to leave Mexico. She planned to drive home. Eventually. Diana had plans to follow the Pacific coastline to California, through the state and then east across the United States.

Her first thought upon entering the States was how much she disliked hearing people. *The language sounds harsh and ugly. I don't want to know what people are saying.*

She slowly made her way through the country. There was a rhythm to it. She would wake and have breakfast and then walk for a few hours. Ideally, this was in the countryside, on a mountain trail or beach, but sometimes it was through towns and villages. She would take in the place. She hiked until she found a calm settle in her. She had bought an iPod and used a computer at a local library to fill it with music. She took it with her on her long treks. Then, she would pack up and drive, get lunch along the way, go for a short stroll, and drive until she found another place to stay. She didn't want to plan where she would be...

I like driving. I like walking. That's all I know. And that ain't much. I guess I also like music. Gillian Welch, Lucinda Williams, Fela Kuti. That's a start. That's something.

There were times like in New York and Big Sur, where she would stay longer because she wanted to explore the place. After a few weeks, she would move on. She was becoming aware that her life had changed. In one of her emails to an old friend, she described her existence.

"This old Ford Granada is struggling. The backseat is serving as a kitchen, library, and closet. It holds a cooler for food, the garbage I toss back there (that is rarely removed), books from second-hand bookstores, and pieces of clothing. It ain't pretty. And it may not smell great."

It was when she received birthday messages that she realized that she had missed it. It was two days after her birthday that she opened the email from Mark with the subject line "HAPPY BIRTHDAY."

I've let this relationship suffer too long. I need to end it. Breaking up feels more like a recognition of a pre-existing condition than an announcement of a new state. He couldn't be surprised. He deserves better. Now, he'll be free to get it.

Her email to him was perfunctory.

"Mark, I'm sorry I've been unavailable to you. And I appreciate your loving patience with me. But it's time we end this. I hope you understand."

She continued travelling for just over six months, until she felt a growing need to go to Toronto. It was a faint tug that grew in strength as the days passed. She allowed herself to be pulled towards it.

She sent an email to Liam to let him know she wanted to come back to her job. She was prepared for him to say no but had a response within a few hours, assuring her that her position was waiting for her whenever she wanted it. She was shocked by this. She never thought Liam cared much for her, and she assumed her sudden departure and prolonged absence had undermined her chances of working with the organization. She was relieved to be wrong.

"Caribou"
Tanya Tagaq

Diana immediately went back to work. In her office, word had spread about what happened to Victoria and how Diana tried to help her. For the first week, she felt the awkward distance between herself and her colleagues. She appreciated and nurtured it.

Liam was the only one to broach the subject with her in those first few days. On that initial afternoon, he stopped by her office. His gait as he walked through her door was measured but awkward.

"It's good to see you, Diana," he announced. She studied his face. It was solemn with an air of concern.

"Thanks." She pushed back from her desk and moved her eyes from her computer screen to meet his.

The silence sat between them. Liam rubbed his lips together and placed his hands on his legs. "It was a tragedy, Diana. Victoria was brave, and like many brave people, she didn't heed the advice of others who were looking out for her safety."

"So, she had it coming?"

"Of course not," said Liam with a slap to the top of his desk. He paused. Inhaled. "What I'm trying to say is that it's not your fault. It's no one's fault."

I thought I was prepared for this. I've thought about this conversation for months. And still, she can get to me. It's her ferocity. It's as though she's always waiting to attack. And she holds this judgment of me. That I'm somehow less committed to the issues. I respect her. We all do. And we feel for her. And all we get is her anger.

Diana stared at him, fuming.

Watch your step, Bishop. Why? I'm not angry with him. Who am I angry with? She searched herself, but she couldn't find the root of her anger.

Of course, I'm still upset that Victoria is gone, and those bastards who murdered her are living unpunished, but this is something more... this is part of it, but there's something else...

Liam could sense she was withdrawing from the fight. He wanted to throw her a rope to pull her out of this. "You know the feds have agreed to let someone from our team go up to PEARL in Nunavut, right?" PEARL was the Polar Environment Atmospheric Research Laboratory in Eureka, Nunavut, which made key measurements to detect and analyze the ozone hole over the Arctic.

"They'll be collecting data, but it would be great to have somebody who can put that in the language for reporting and for the media, and to figure out the political spin. Interested?"

Diane instinctively knew she was interested. She knew she was going to do it. But part of her didn't want to agree with Liam. "It's just to start it up, right?"

"Yeah, you could head up in early March and stay until the fall."

"Well, maybe... Okay." Diana loved the idea of being busy, travelling, being away from everything.

Just under two months later, Diana was making her way east to catch a flight from CFB Trenton to Alert. As she sat on the train travelling along Lake Ontario, she grew anxious with each passing kilometer beyond Oshawa. The landscape began to look like the place where she started her life. It had been twenty-five years since she left here on a train. Now, she was going back on a train so she could leave again — this time on a plane. The irony of it made her both laugh a little and feel sad. A hollowness was creeping into her. She looked up, pressed the button for the attendant. As he arrived at her seat, she turned to him. "May I have two of your little bottles of wine, please?"

As she flew, she was taken aback by the harsh beauty of the North. It was March, and the sun was just starting to show itself after a winter of darkness. There was a constant light that made the land and everything else glow. It sent a chill through her with its grave beauty.

She spent a day in meetings and then travelled to the research station from Alert. Only a small group were staying at the station. She was happy to have the space and constant traffic of new people coming in and out of Alert.

Diana dove into her work. There was little else to do there. To protect her free time from being overcome with social obligations, she announced that she was a big reader and would spend evenings in her small room, listening to the wind howl around it. It brought her a sort of peace.

As late spring grew and summer appeared, she spent more time outdoors. The sun circled overhead through the day and the night never setting, just rolling around the sky like a ball inside a small plastic container of a child's game.

The spring was like winter in southern Canada, and the summer was like early spring, with temperatures rising above and dipping below freezing. But there was hardly any rain.

She would escape to be outside whenever possible and would work with her laptop. Her colleagues found her solitary nature odd. She sensed it. Before leaving, she started to announce herself: "I need a wide berth to roam."

She paused to listen to the water dashing in the rivers from the thaw. She closed her eyes and felt a delicate touch of warmth from the sun. She opened them to see the mountain ranges in the distance.

This emptiness reminds me of the deserts of California, Arizona, and New Mexico. It is a desert, I guess—a desert with fjords.

She brushed her hand along the top of the small, low flowers—arctic poppies and forget-me-nots that would live in the brief summer afforded here. Diana liked to sit still and remain quiet. It allowed the wildlife to feel at ease, and she would be more likely to see them.

Will you come back to me, my wolves? Can I join your pack? She smiled to herself.

One evening in August, she returned to their base in Eureka. She knew it was time for her to leave. Lucy, a researcher, had told her that a massive storm was striking the Gulf Coast. Diana joined others gathered around the TV to watch the reporting on CNN. She had never seen an American city flooded like this. The wall alongside a levy in New Orleans had broken, and water was pouring into the community beside it. Beneath it, really. It had formed a small lake that was already over six feet high. Cars had been swallowed up, homes were flooded, and people were drowning in what they said was the Ninth Ward of the city.

For six months now, she had been at a research station in the Arctic Circle. It calmed her. The work was monotonous, reading reports and pulling information out of the scientists. The end of her work was nearing. The need for change was growing in her.

She knew New Orleans and that area were struck with seasonal storms, but everyone said the strength of this one was unique, and the city had been unprepared. The phrase that kept going through her mind was "man-made catastrophe." Someone on TV had said that at around 2:00 a.m. The levees were not built to withstand the storms they knew were coming, let alone this one. It was bigger than most. The US Army Corps of Engineers, who were responsible for levees, were unapologetic. A warning had been issued for people to leave the city. Of course, most had. The most vulnerable were still there: those with no cars, no money, or no means to get reliable information.

She was drawn to it. She knew she had to go down there. She knew she had to help them. A strength rose in her that hadn't been there in a long time. She felt renewed.

I don't need to look to the sky tonight to know what I have to do.

"Under The Milky Way"
The Church

It was after Diana decided to go to New Orleans that I began my search for her. There were reports of her online but little in the way of contact information. She didn't have a Facebook account. Searching her name, I came across a post by Francine, her childhood friend. Her full name was Francine Chisamore. She had written a birthday post for Diana that mentioned her by name. Francine was living in the Scott's Mills area. So, I reached out to her.

Devin
Hi Francine, we haven't met, but I'm trying to get in touch with people who may know Diana Glendon. I met Diana a long time ago and was trying to get in touch with her again.

Francine
Hi Devin, why do you want information about Diana?

Devin
Thanks for your response. Diana was involved in an accident years ago. I was also in it. I've finally been dealing with it, and I hoped to get in touch with her.

Francine
What accident was that? And are you okay?

Devin
When she was 18, in 1978, she was involved in an accident in Scott's Mills. I'm fine.

Francine
Okay. I think I know all about this. Someone died in that accident, didn't they? A little boy.

Devin
Yeah. He did pass away. It was just a terrible accident. It must have been awful for her, as well.

Francine
I'm sorry if I sound suspicious, but Diana has angered a lot of bad people in her life, and I'm always afraid that someone will try and dig up information about her to hurt her or something. I probably sound crazy.

Devin
No, don't worry. I understand. I should tell you that I was with him. The boy who died. He was my friend. But I wasn't harmed.

Francine
Oh no. I'm so sorry. She told me she had hit a child on a bike that was too big for him. She went to a house and got blankets to cover him and keep him warm. I don't remember much more except that he had passed away. She said the police involved were very kind.

Devin
Yes, that's the accident. I just wanted to find her so we could talk about it. It's haunted me, and I'm sure it's troubled her, as well.

Francine
Well, I'm sure she would like to talk to you. It may be hard, though.

Devin
Why?

Francine
She went to the Arctic Circle for work!

Devin
Whoa. That would be tough then.

Francine

Yeah. I miss her. She was my best friend. I haven't seen her since the accident. She just disappeared after that. I wanted to be there for her. I've reached out to her over the years. I just don't know what to offer. I don't know what she's looking for. She's not great on email and doesn't have a cell phone. Anyway, she's working on a project called PEARL. I only know because I try to keep track of her. If you look into that, I'm sure you can get a message to her.

Devin
Okay. Thanks again.

Francine
You're welcome. Can you let me know if you find her? And if you do, let her know that I would love to hear from her.

Devin
For sure.

That was early March in 2007. I sent the message to the project lead, and two days later, I had a response.

Hello, Devin,

Thanks for your message, but I'm sorry to report that Diana has left. Our only knowledge of her was that she wanted to volunteer in the emergency response to Hurricane Katrina on the Gulf Coast over a year ago.

Kind regards,
Lesley Faber
PEARL Manager of Operations.

I could see the patterns of her life forming before me. She was alone and headed into danger. She was choosing it. Of course, my perspective on Diana would be skewed as our encounter would always be the lens through which she would be seen. And she seemed to be doing what I had done—

putting herself at risk to purge shame, or challenge death, or at least say her piece.

As I learned more about her, I worried that the accident was still unresolved for her. I was then twice the age of that poor girl who had a part to play in that tragedy. And I didn't know if anyone had told her that it wasn't her fault. That it was just a terrible accident. Was the wound only growing over the years? Time does not always heal. It can deepen the trauma and spread it until it overtakes our lives and leave us worse, if it's not dressed. The only method I've known is addressing it directly: sitting with the memories and growing nauseous, angry, despairing and letting that out.

I could feel the part of me that has always needed to protect and save the vulnerable, injured, and outcast. I didn't trust it. I knew I was trying to "save" someone who hadn't asked for it. It was only recently that I finally realized that the amount of arrogance that kind of thing required, and it was pretty shocking. It was also misguided. I, of course, was only trying to save them because I couldn't protect my friend when we were kids. And maybe by helping them, I could release myself from the shame for what happened that day.

But I was done with that. Sean's death wasn't my fault. I did nothing wrong. And neither did she. And I wanted to make sure Diana knew that. If I were her, I would like to hear that. I packed up a few things and left for New Orleans. May understood. I felt compelled to do it. I pushed onwards, as though part of me knew I needed to rush to get there.

"Wish Someone Would Care"
Irma Thomas

Diana had been in the city for a year and a half. She was staying in a long narrow house the locals called a "shotgun". "If all the doors are open, a shotgun blast fired into it from the front doorway will fly cleanly to the other end and out at the back," the guy who rented it to her told her when she asked about the name. It was just north of the French Quarter, in the Tremé neighbourhood.

She had spent her first few months with others cleaning up damage in the city. Eventually, she had been hired through Catholic Charities as a coordinator for the return of residents in the Lafitte Housing Projects. The windows and doors of the substantial brick buildings in the project were covered with a heavy plastic that was bolted to the structure. This was done to stop access to the homes. Some of the residents had evacuated, and those that hadn't were forced to leave and barred from returning to the buildings.

Officials had said that the homes were "unsafe" after the storm. Diana had been fighting against this stance. From the outside, the homes appeared undisturbed by the storm. Local residents echoed this and reported little damage. Their statements were largely ignored.

She had learned the history and had befriended residents who let her know the full story. This public housing project was sitting on prized real estate, being just a little north of the French Quarter — the centre of tourism for the city. The housing projects had been the first ones dedicated to black people when they launched. About ten years before the storm, the homes were slated for demolition, but the community fought back and the plan was cancelled.

Now, Diana was aware those plans were once again afoot. The argument some government staff and developers were making was that the residents had fled, and now they couldn't come back to these homes because they were unsafe.

So, it was best that the houses were demolished and a new community should take its place. Diana and other housing advocates had fought to ensure that the occupants could come back home. The officials conceded that if someone could put together a list of these people and how they could be contacted, they would be invited back.

For months, Diana pulled together information and spoke to residents to find out where people were after the storm. She tracked them down at their relatives and at hotels, told them her plan and collected their information. Sometimes she went in person to find people. She travelled across Louisiana and as far as Houston, Atlanta, and Baltimore. She now had the names and contact information for over a thousand residents.

In New Orleans, the word was out about this woman from Canada stirring up things in the Laffite. Diana had heard about other people being threatened, attacked, and killed in these chaotic months after the storm. At times, she had the feeling she was being watched. Her colleagues and friends warned her that she was in danger, and so was her plan.

"You know, down here these days, information and people go missing all the time. They don't play by your rules," warned Cassandra. She was a leader of a group forming an NGO to ensure there was housing for low-income people. It gave Diana pause. But as the developers pressured the government and its agencies, the rhetoric around crime in the deserted community grew, and destruction of the homes was posed as the only solution. Diana felt she needed to do something.

It's gotta be big and draw media attention. That's the only way we can fight them.

Cassandra's words were in her head as she drove through the night in the city. She sighed, thinking about how much she loved New Orleans, especially in the autumn. She made her way across Basin Street, past Congo Square, and on to Orleans Avenue. She slowed her Jeep as she reached the edge of the Lafitte projects. The neighbourhood was deserted. Quiet. It made her feel uneasy, and she responded by turning her thoughts away from it and moved to action. She hopped out of the Jeep and made her way towards the property. She paused and then turned back towards the vehicle and pulled out chain-link cutters and a crowbar.

Let's go, let's go, just get it done... It's just too friggin' quiet. Sing. My darlin' New Orlins, my brawlin' hometown... Your magnolia melancholy, how it softly sets me down... There we go.

She cut through the fence at an unlit spot. The recently installed security lights had burned out in this location. The others were still on, so as soon as she made it through the barrier, she could be seen if anyone was near. She pulled the wire patch away and pushed herself through it. She felt an urge to look back but didn't, and sprinted towards the housing development. Up close, she was surprised the solid buildings showed little, if any, signs of the storm.

She saw the heavy plastic bolted on doors and windows to make sure nobody could get into the homes. She quickly went to work with the crowbar on one of the doors. It was hard and noisy work. She went bolt by bolt, pulling at the plastic, cursing under her breath and sweating in the warm night. She removed the covering from one side of the door, slipped her hand through and reached the door handle. It was locked. But with a few tries with the crowbar, she popped the door open. She climbed past the covering, through the open door, and into the room.

She scanned the home. It had an open concept with the kitchen looking into a living room. It smelled a little musty but there were no signs of water damage. "Unbelievable," she muttered. "They made these poor people move for no damn reason. It's true. They just wanted them out."

She pulled out her phone to take photos of the room and realized even with the security lights outside, it really wasn't bright enough. She turned on the flash on her phone. Diana didn't try the lights. She assumed they wouldn't work as the power company likely cut power to the homes. From the moment she arrived, she was surprised at how calm she felt.

I could live here, in a home like this, in New Orleans. Maybe stop rambling and build a life here. This place is probably one of the few places that would know what to do with me. I'm useful here, and maybe they even like me a little.

She walked around the house, snapping pictures. It was so tidy and clearly loved. She saw that there was a turntable with a bunch of albums on a shelf beside it, along with a big comfy chair.

The fact that someone put these two things together makes me like this unknown person. Listening to old records in a big comfy chair in the Lafitte Tremé in New Orleans. That sounds good to me. She smiled.

Scanning the records, Diana pulled out an Irma Thomas album, "Wish Someone Would Care." Friends in the city had turned her on to Irma. She placed the record on the deck of the turntable.

I'll give it a try. I like the process anyway.

She was surprised to see the turntable respond. The power must be on in here, she thought. She turned on the receiver.

I love that scratchy sound at the start of a record.

"Cry, cry
Sitting home alone, thinkin' about my past
Wonderin' how I made it, and how long it's gonna last..."

Her mind returned to her purpose. Diana turned down the music. She pulled out her phone and started to record a video. "I'm in unit twenty-two of the Lafitte Housing Projects with Irma Thomas. The place is fine. No reason a person couldn't live here. I know I would love to call this home." She scanned the room with the phone. She finished and texted it to a reporter she knew at the Times-Picayune, Max Simon. "Come on by, Max. I've gotta show you something."

She sat down in the chair beside the stereo in the living room. She spread the documents across her lap. It was the list of residents. She started the song again, leaned back in the comfy chair and closed her eyes.

The song was just ending when a bright red light appeared in her eyes and then a terrible sound, a push and a hot feeling in her chest. She knew what had happened. She opened her eyes. Darkness quickly grew around her sightlines. She felt like she was floating. She was surprised how little it hurt. It just seemed to be an overwhelming of her senses with conflicting data: hot-and-cold-light-and-dark-sadness-and-ease... and then just ease.

"Take My Hand, Precious Lord"
Mahalia Jackson

I was still travelling to New Orleans when I got the news.

I had driven from my home on Cashell Island. I wanted time to prepare myself to meet Diana, and travelling by car afforded that. I had passed through the northern states that seem like a reflection of Canada—Michigan and Ohio. I stayed at a little motel by the highway in Ohio for the night. The next day, I moved on to Kentucky, Tennessee, and now Mississippi. I was going to stop for the night in Jackson. I had covered a lot of ground, having driven about eleven hours. I was only about 200 miles from New Orleans, which meant I could get there by lunch tomorrow after a good night's sleep. It was my first time in the deep south. There was something exotic and compelling about it. There was also a persistent whiff of uncertainty and danger.

I thought of May. I was guarded. I had a lot on my plate, dealing with all of this and being a single parent. But she was understanding, kind, and loving. Right now, she was worried about me. I knew I needed to keep speaking about what happened to me and what I was doing now. So, when I arrived in Jackson and settled into my hotel, I sent her an email.

I've been travelling along the muddy, not as mighty as I expected, Mississippi River. For Americans, it's one of their first highways, I guess. I never thought of that before. Here, that murky river widens into a delta. The land is rich and the people poor. Soils and water mix and bigotry struggles to carry on. It seems trapped in history. This land is so rich and beautiful, but there is no ease or healing in these alluvial plains. Maybe it's just because I arrived in Jackson to hear news reports about the trial of white men who killed a black man outside a convenience store. A father, who had a box of diapers in his hands. A box of diapers. They tied him up behind their truck and drove until he died. They left his body in a segregated cemetery. Then they went out for a barbecue. I read and shuddered.

234

I had a fitful sleep, so I let myself sleep in a little late. When I finally woke up around 11:00 a.m., I was eager to get going. I picked up the car and went to a gas station before having a late breakfast. The man behind the counter there noticed my accent.

"Where you from?"

"Canada."

"What you doing down here?"

"Heading to New Orleans to see about a friend."

"Well, that poor town is rough now."

"Yeah. Seems rough everywhere."

The man fell silent.

I arrived at the restaurant, ordered breakfast, pulled out my computer and was about to go to the website for the New Orleans Times-Picayune. I wanted to know a little more about where I was going, so I had started reading the newspaper online each morning. On the homepage, there was the story about Diana. The title read "Local Activist Shot During Break and Enter in Lafitte Projects."

I was stunned. I read it a few times before it sunk in. I looked around me like I wanted to tell someone. I didn't really know her, but grief overcame me. I felt like I lost an aunt or a sister. I had recently taught myself to let it happen to me, even here in a diner in Mississippi. I sat at my table and wept for her death and for my failure in reaching her and saving her. I wept for not being able to tell her that it wasn't her fault. I wept for the damage she had done that could not now be undone. I wept for the damage done to her. I wept for feeling alone in it now. There were three of us that day. Now there was just me. I felt so tired, weak, and worn. So, I continued to weep.

My face was soaked with tears and snot. I held my head in my hands, trying to control myself. I made embarrassing sounds. My waitress, Pearl, came by my table. She topped up my coffee and placed a hand on my shoulder.

"Those that don't grieve, suffer," she offered, paused and moved on.

I tried to mutter a "Thank you" and continued to cry.

"At The Foot of Canal Street"
John Boutte

I wasn't sure what to do now that I heard Diana was gone, but I wanted to finish what I had started. Eventually, I got myself together, paid up, packed up, and started my drive through the Mississippi Delta down to New Orleans. I took my time and stopped a few times for short walks and dinner. I arrived in the city just after eight in the evening.

The drive along the river and to New Orleans brought a growing intensity. I was haunted, agitated, and unhappy. As I crossed the bridge over Lake Pontchartrain, the city greeted me with an assault to the senses. It was a warm autumn night. I should have enjoyed the weather, but when I opened the windows of the car, the smells of decay, and death flowed into the vehicle.

The streets were deserted. The homes that were once as colourful as a horn solo, were now muted with chipped paint, and spray-painted by unseen hands. The air was wet, the moon swam. All that was displayed by the weak, remaining streetlights were the broken remnants of the city. Damaged homes, busted cars, garbage, and deserted schools. My anger and fear were rising. But I refused to allow myself to feel panic. I wanted to stomp out all of this darkness. I wanted to fight it.

After making it through Metairie and Mid-City, I arrived in the Tremé. I found the Lafitte projects and searched until I saw the building from the news reports. There was no one on the street. The sky was dark and cloudy, and the orange streetlights glared at me. I got out of my car and circled the property. The tall fence reminded me of the barriers you would see at prisons. My outrage grew. The news reports had stated that Diana was a housing activist who believed these homes shouldn't be destroyed because they had minimal damage, and the residents should be allowed to come back to them. I understood her stance, and I shared it.

I remembered that I drove by one military vehicle on my way into the city, a Humvee with soldiers in camouflage. I had read that the National Guard was still present and would be for some time to come. It seemed like the city could use soldiers with shovels and hammers more than guns.

As I continued to circle the property, I came across a hole in the fence. Police tape swayed in the light breeze, making the only noise. But I didn't feel alone. I peered through the opening, fuming. Would I go in there? What could I do? Who could I fight? And then I stopped. A breeze blew up around me. A voice whispered, "Your anger will kill you."

I felt useless and restless. I had been unsettled for thirty years. I bounced off everything in my life, or flew above it, or ran from it. I could end that now. If I entered that building, I might not emerge from it. I could fight, maybe one last time and end my struggle. I gazed into the dark, sweating. I wanted this pain to end...

An image of Lily surfaced and then May. And then me. I was writing these words. It mattered. I could have a life if I let myself. I could feel the strength of that thought rising in me.

I turned away and walked back to my car. I found the address for my hotel, drove there, checked in and dropped my bag in my room. I wandered the French Quarter and into Marigny. The odours persisted, but there was so much spectacular music and revelry on Frenchman Street that I felt lifted. I wandered from bar to bar drinking bourbon on the rocks until I grew tired.

Back at my hotel, I laid on the bed and opened my computer. I went to my Facebook account. I needed to tell Francine. She needed to hear from a friend that Diana had passed away.

The green dot appeared beside her name that let me know she was online.

Devin
Francine? Are you there?

Francine
Hi. Yes.

Devin
How are you?

Francine
I'm okay. I have insomnia, so I only sleep for two hours at a time. It comes in waves and has been terrible recently.

Devin
Sorry to hear that.

Francine
It's okay. It's part of being a healer. I'm so sensitive that it's difficult to sleep.

Devin
You're a healer?

Francine
Yes, did I not tell you that?

Devin
No.

Francine
Yes, I can sense the often-hidden pain in people and animals. I find animals more open to healing, so I help them. If I'm

honest, I always hoped Diana would come back to me, and I could help her. Maybe I could heal her. It's part of the reason I've set myself up like this.
Devin
That's interesting. It's good to have a calling.

Francine
It's just who I am.

Devin
(I knew I needed to tell her about Diana. She needed to hear it from someone who cared about Diana and could be there for her when she got the news.)
Did you hear about Diana?

Francine
Hear what?

Devin
Do you want to speak on the phone?

Francine
Oh my god! I haven't been able to sleep the last two nights. I knew something was wrong with someone in my orbit. Is she okay?

Devin
Well, no. Would you like to speak on the phone?

Francine
No. It's better this way.

Devin
She passed away in New Orleans.

Francine

AIN'T NOTHIN' BUT A STRANGER IN THIS WORLD

Oh, my God.

Devin
I'm sorry.

Francine
What happened?

Devin
Do you want me to send news reports?

Francine
Okay. [I sent her the links, and she responded a few minutes later.] So violent. My poor Diana.

Devin
What can I do for you?

Francine
Nothing. I have to go.

Devin
Francine, I know something about how you feel right now. It's not your fault. There's nothing you could have done. There's nothing any of us could have done. I know because I'm here in New Orleans. I came to find her. I'm always here if you want to talk.

Francine
You are? I'm so sorry. All these years I've waited for her to come back. To help her. Now, that will never happen.

Devin
Are you sure you don't want to talk?

Francine.
No. I need to go. Thank you. Good night.

I closed my computer and immediately fell asleep.

I woke in the morning with these thoughts: I had come to the city to find a person and offer forgiveness, and if I'm honest, seek it. Even from the driver of the vehicle that day. Part of me wanted her to tell me it wasn't my fault.

I was feeling low, so I did what everyone who feels sad does in New Orleans: I walked down to the Mississippi River to follow along its banks. I didn't walk far before I set myself down like a heavy bag. I sat on a bench watching the waters pass by me with its big boats moving to and fro.

I wanted relief from myself. An older man, maybe sixty, in a light suit and with dark skin, sat down beside me. He turned to me and began to speak: "You just throw your troubles into that river. That's what the Mississippi is here for, friend."

I looked at him, surprised. I merely nodded in return.

"You know that New Orleans is a place where all of our paths end?"

I said nothing. I was too far within myself to find words. But he had my attention. I turned to him.

"Some people need an ending, and it's often afforded to them here."

A teenager on a skateboard came by, stepped on the end of his board to kick it up, grabbed it, and looked at me. "She did it for us, but she also did it for herself. She chose this."

A child no more than two years old looked at me from her stroller as her mother pushed it. The little girl in her white linen dress leaned forward and nodded her head. She leaned back as her mother continued walking.

I sat in dumbfounded silence. The skateboarder continued: "It's okay to grieve. It's okay to want something different for her. But you have to accept what she chose. This was her life." He dropped his board and pushed off.

I quit thinking and sobbed.

A young woman with a guitar who had been sitting and playing on the steps to the Mississippi river, now walked by. She put a hand on my shoulder.

"She would've liked you. She does like you." She turned away and started playing her guitar and singing: "This city won't wash away..."

The old man got up and started walking away.

"Thank you," I stammered to him and to the young woman.

"You'll be okay," he offered. He threw me a broad smile and a wave. He hollered over his shoulder, "We'll take care of ya."

And he was right. Wherever I went the rest of that day and night in New Orleans, people smiled and engaged me kindly. No one would let me pay for anything at the music clubs on Frenchmen Street. I stepped into DBA's, and I was talking to some people who had bought me a bourbon at the bar when John Boutté took the stage. He spoke to the crowd. "This is for our Canadian friend in the house, and his friend, who found a home in New Orleans." And then he sang "At The Foot Of Canal Street."

Just before John began to sing, I raised a glass to Diana. "To Diana!" I hollered. The crowd responded, "Diana!" Tears of relief trickled down my face knowing that she found a home. She found her rest, and she would not be forgotten. Her life mattered.

"I'll see you there (at the foot of Canal Street).
What will you wear (at the foot of Canal Street)?
Will the band be playing (at the foot of Canal Street)?
What will the people be saying (at the foot of Canal Street)?

Does your father lie there?
Does your mother pray there?
I'm gonna lay my burdens down,
I'm going to put on my golden Crown,
I'm moving up to higher ground,
At the foot of Canal Street."

"The Way Young Lovers Do"
Van Morrison

It was just before dawn that I made it back to my room. I sent May an email. I wrote to her about all of this and added more:

> *I fell in love with New Orleans tonight. It's strange, maybe odd and a little daft, to love a city the way I do, but to love without any sense of irony is always foolish, they say. I'm committed to being a fool for New Orleans. I'm pleased to be a fool for you, too.*

> *I don't know how I could deny the city and its people. Here the waters meet: the Mississippi rolls into the ocean. The land is mixed with water but doesn't form a forgettable mud. This is the fallow ground. Indigenous, Spanish, West African, French, English, Korean, Irish, American... The world has traversed these streets. The people of this place are hope for us. They are the enemies of nothing at all, able to allow themselves to live alongside the spiced, churning waters of life, creating and creating and creating to honour the best in us. It is a city that, when it sleeps, must dream of itself. I love walking the streets late at night. New Orleans sighs and exhales these notions and I receive them as precious gifts...*

> *This is the primordial soup from which we sprung. This is the act of creation, the chance to be renewed, to no longer struggle against oneself. When any of us are fractured or lost, New Orleans will receive us. And from its waters and coaxed by its words and sounds, we can be healed if we allow ourselves. I'm sure of it.*

> *When my thoughts wander to Diana and how I didn't save her, the city laughs at me tenderly. It whispers to me as I walk the French Quarter just before dawn: "write and keep writing..."*

> *Great loss and its pain is a pathway to meaning. You finally chose to travel it and found yourself, your gifts and what you can offer this world. And that is your joy. It is a great irony —*

245

travelling into our wound is maybe the only way we can find some sort of sustainable happiness.

> *May, I believe it. Knowing that, and having a language that I've denied for so long, is the gift I need to give myself permission to receive. I can offer a handful of shining words and my joyful dedication to you. It may not be as much as others can offer, but it may be the best of me. I love you.*

"Madame George"
Van Morrison

Back home on Cashell Island, the warm summer day turns into night. I sit at my desk, with a touch of light around me from the lamp, while in the next room I hear my eldest child sigh and move into sleep like the geese leaving the earth for flight outside my window. Yes, my eldest, as we now have another daughter. Just a baby. Siobhán.

The water steps lightly onto the shore. There are only a few of us in the twenty-five square miles of rocky shoreline, meadows, and forests. And we all like it that way. We have a shared privacy.

I am happy to be alone in my limestone coach house with a sleeping child. Our play today is done. Mudpies are drying in the yard. I can see May move through our house collecting the day. Out my window, the night grows starry. The world slackens.

I'm jolted by howling. It's the Akbash guard dogs in our neighbour's field. Protecting the lambs in the night. They're tracking down a coyote that's hunting the lambs. The wild sounds of the dogs give way to a climactic confrontation between predators and their prey. In the final stage of the chase, I hear the pursued animal turn to face its attackers and temporarily repel the dogs, rendering them only to stand and wail. Keeping them at bay before the end. I understand this language of growls and yelps, the clenched muscles and the teeth standing in the moonlight. These are their words:

"Howl for a childhood friend killed in front of you. Howl of your burden and shame. Howl for the indifference towards suffering. And howl to keep everyone at bay, for you know you are too often only desperate teeth. You are the anger that would attack anything. So, you feast on distance and the dark. Alone with your shame for not being able to save what's been lost. Howl into your ending..."

247

The island is quiet now. The fight is over. I shudder.
But I know I am no longer the coyote or the guard dogs. But I
understand both and know that to shudder in their presence
is all I need to do now. The moon glows. The child continues
to sleep. My wife turns off the lights in the house.

As you know, in this story, I am Devin. Though I was
also Alexander. I was called to write, and that voice that led
me to these words on the page was Sean. He has been with me
since his intrusion a few years ago. I finally let myself be near
him and listen. It was a generous gift from my friend to come
back to me.

Since that day, I've been writing for my life. I was
scribbling to find a way back into life. To live. And then I
found my happiness.

Sean smiles.

When we were swallowed by the trauma and all of
our shame, hope, fear, guilt, madness, and purpose, we
claimed it was because of Sean. But he is only one person. And
that person is just a boy of six. He did not choose to die that
day but also didn't decide to have this role. And he led me to
write, and back to myself. This sweet child let us know that
we are forgiven, we are loved, and we must let him go so he
may be a spirit in peace. We can still know him and feel his
presence, but we can no longer burden him with our needs.

Who am I to say Sean's life was anything other than
what he *knew* it to be? It may have only been six years, but that
was his life and to mourn it is to undermine the meaning it
had for him. *His* life. Not mine. My wishes for it are my own,
and they should have no more bearing in his death than they
would when he was here with us. They were my hopes, and
they are a breeze on any day. Passing only. My grief was my
choice, and it was about me. I am done with it. Instead, I

celebrate my friend. It was Diana that taught me to do that. And I praise her, as well. I love them both.

On my finest days now, I live in a moment from one of my favourite songs, when Van Morrison is circling in transcendence, chanting:

> "And the love that loves to love
> That loves to love
> That loves to love
> That loves to love
> The love that loves to love
> That love that loves..."

In a phrase, maybe all of this sadness of mine was love unawakened.

I remember that it's early August, and the Swift-Tuttle comet is passing by the Earth. Friends have told me that it's the most massive object known to repeatedly pass by the planet, creating the annual Perseid meteor shower. Tonight, all the darkness will be broken by lights travelling at nearly sixty kilometers a second.

These objects may be classified as debris, but at the moment they enter our atmosphere, they become a moment of light. We have greater visibility of this meteor shower at this distance than from the cities and towns. So, I leave the coach house and walk away from the glow of home. Finding a spot along the shore, I wait for the comet.

I feel like a child. I sit in the dark, but I sense the light in everything around me. Its source and meaning are only partially understood. They are still a puzzle to me. And I'm at ease with not knowing more. In fact, the mystery of it all sustains me now.

Tonight, and always in this place, a great lake feeds a river that flows out to the ocean. In the moonlight, I watch it. The movement is so slow it's almost imperceptible. I watch it move on to something greater than what it once was. Tonight, I watch it as a
grateful guest in this land called peace.

Sean Michael Ross

I was born on May 17, 1972. My given name is Sean Michael Ross. I received a mother, a father, and two sisters. And a best friend.

For all of my years, I dwelt in the village of Scott's Mills, Ontario. I've loved life. Most days, I felt a warmth in my chest like glowing coals from a fire were within me. Even when I passed away, this feeling never left me, and I suppose that's who I am.

Some of my favourite things were: making mud pies, watching the river form rapids behind my house in the spring, riding my bike, LEGO and making people laugh.

Sometimes I get bored. Then I would hear questions in my head? "Who am I? Am I really separate from everything around me? Why am I here in this place now?"

The day I graduated from kindergarten, I was travelling home on my older sister's bike with Devin. He got off the bike to avoid his mother's gaze. When I started again, I was struck by a truck. I died moments later.

When I was five years old, my parents took me to the lakeshore in the autumn. Lake Ontario's waters had dropped, revealing large slabs of limestone that were no longer beneath the waves. Hundreds of millions of years ago, they were at the bottom of a tropical sea, south of here. The land migrated north to this place with the rest of the continent.

There were mountains just north of us many years ago. The glaciers toppled them and then retreated, leaving us the lake that lay over the limestone. On the lake bed's exposed rock surface are impressions of creatures and plants from that ancient sea. I sat down to touch the markings. I lay my cheek against the grooves of the warm stone. It was as old as anything I would ever know. This stone whispered to me of what it knew, and now that is what I know.

ACKNOWLEDGEMENTS

I would like to thank my dear partner, Carrie, for her steadfast support and love. I would also like to thank Sandra Gulland and Mark Sampson for their insightful notes on the manuscript, along with the Editors at Ace of Swords Publishing for their belief in the book and their valuable feedback.

ABOUT THE AUTHOR

Bruce Sudds is a graduate of York University with a specialization in Creative Writing. He has worked as a journalist, speech writer and social entrepreneur.

Bruce does most of his scribbling on an island near Kingston, Ontario, Canada, where he lives with his wife, Carrie, and their three daughters.

Manufactured by Amazon.ca
Bolton, ON